THE HOLLYWOOD **BOOK NINEEEN** MURDER MYSTERIES
1965

# ASHES TO ASHES

# PETER S. FISCHER

www.petersfischer.com

Ashes to Ashes

ISBN 978-0-9960491-8-4

*To my grandson, Nicholas—*
*making his way in the world with ambition*
*and good humor despite the caprices of Fate.*

# PROLOGUE

The first warning sign occurred two weeks ago. I was at my desk typing away, deep into Chapter Seventeen of my new novel, an adventure thriller set in a Colorado ski lodge in the dead of winter. I had been working non-stop for almost seven weeks, holed up in my office, drinking coffee early in the day and Coors after three o'clock. Carelessly I had knocked my empty coffee cup off my desk onto the carpeted floor. Luckily it didn't break but when I leaned down to pick it up, I suddenly felt a severe muscle pull in my side. I gasped in pain, tried to straighten up to no avail, then got to my feet and tried to stretch it out, rubbing it vigorously. It took several minutes for it to disappear and I could resume sitting in my chair. I knew right away what the problem was. For weeks I had been sedentary and without exercise of any kind, carrying an extra eight pounds of fat and feeling every one of my 45 years. Sleep was beginning to elude me and tingly stabs of discomfort were attacking my legs and feet. I knew what was wrong and knew what I had to do, no matter how lazy I was feeling or how preoccupied I was with the book. I had to get out into the world and put my body back together again.

The next morning I'd arisen around six thirty, donned sweats and sneakers and then left the house, determined to do a half-hour walk at a brisk pace. At minute sixteen, on a very slight incline, I felt a stabbing pain in my left side. Oh, God no, I thought, not a heart attack and I sat down on the curb to collect myself. If I moved the wrong way, the stabbing pain reasserted itself. Minutes passed and eventually I could move easily. The crisis had passed for the moment. I headed for home and when I got to my office, I called Lev Rosen, my doctor of twelve years. When I told him what I'd gone through, he told me to haul my bloated ass to his office right after lunch and he would squeeze me in.

He started by tapping my chest and then my back. Cough, please. Thank you. Then out of his refrigerator came the chilled stethoscope which enabled him to eavesdrop on every hidden cranny of my body. He peered into my eyes and my ears, saying nothing, merely grunting to himself. Finally he tells me to put my shirt back on and then come down the hall to his office. This is in direct contrast to what he usually says which is,'You're fine. Go home. Kiss your wife. I'll see you next year'.

A couple of minutes later I found him at his desk busily working on some forms.

"So, am I sick?" I'd asked.

"Of course you're sick," he'd said. "Why else would you be here?"

"I'm not sure I'm really sick. Doc. Just out of shape."

"So now you're a doctor. And without even medical school. Congratulations." He hands me a piece of paper. "Take this straight to UCLA med center. I've ordered a couple of tests."

"What kind of tests?"

"I'll call them and tell them you're coming. I want these tests done today."

"What's the matter with me, Doc? You act like I'm dying."

"You're not dying, not yet. That's why we do the tests. I'm also referring you to Jim McCaffrey. He's a cardiologist. I'll set something up in the next day or two."

"So it's my heart," I say, confirming my worst fear.

"Excuse me, my know-it-all friend,but that's the purpose of the tests," Lev said to me just before throwing me out of his office.

So I went to the Medical Center at UCLA and had my tests and met Jim McCaffrey who dropped by at Lev's request and a couple of days later I was in McCaffrey's office, getting the official verdict.

"Atherosclerosis."

"What the hell is that?"

"In laymen's terms, hardening of the arteries. Your case is moderate and we can treat it with medicine and a change of diet."

"Not sure I like that last part," I'd said.

"Beats the hell out of no diet at all," McCaffrey opined. "Let me guess. You're partial to red meat and lots of it, tons of butter on your potatoes and vegetables if you actually eat vegetables, which I doubt. Then there's the pizza and the cheeseburgers and maybe beer."

"Amen."

"All of which are clogging your arteries, setting you up for a stroke or a heart attack."

"I see," I'd said, "but if I eat my lettuce and carrots and brussel sprouts like a good little boy, I could live to be a hundred. Is that the sales pitch, Doc?"

"I'm not Merlin, Mr. Bernardi, so you'll never live to be a hundred but you've got a shot at eighty if you behave yourself which means you could see your daughter married and maybe collect a few grandchildren and also enjoy a well earned retirement but of course, that's all up to you."

Up to me. I loved the way he put it. You want to live, pal? Get used to iceberg lettuce and tomatoes and onions and forget about New York steaks and New Zealand lamb chops and juicy burgers and cold beers on a warm summer day.

"Now let's talk about exercise," McCaffrey continues. Uh,oh. Not my favorite subject. "If you've been avoiding it, better get started. Very light to start. A twenty minute brisk walk, okay. If you've got a treadmill, use it. Twenty minutes in the swimming pool would be excellent. A few laps, slow paced. You're not training for the Olympics. Whatever you do, no heavy exertion. I mean that, Joe. Don't try to fix your problem all at once. Slow and steady. I'll see you back here in three weeks and we'll reevaluate."

I nod compliantly. I like the idea of swimming laps in the pool but walking a treadmill? What could be more boring?

I also have another problem and her name is Bunny. Luckily my loving wife has her own doctor, a woman with a private practice near the newspaper office where she works as an editor so she won't be inadvertently learning anything from Lev Rosen. Here's how I look at it. The particulars of my health are on a need-to-know basis and Bunny doesn't need to know. When I cheat and order a steak at Chasen's or sneak a few bottles of beer, I don't want to have to deal with constant wailing and moaning about how I am trying to kill myself and leave Bunny a widow and Yvette fatherless. If I am lucky and cut back and faithfully take my medicine, I may beat this thing and a few months or so from now I may be my old self again.

After my meeting with McCaffrey I went immediately home and slipped into a pair of seldom used, much too tight swim trunks and hopped into the pool. I did two leisurely laps, back and forth twice, before I decided I'd had enough. My arms and legs were heavy and my breathing wasn't all that great. I was just climbing out of the pool when Bunny appeared in the sliding doorway, totally bewildered by my behavior, knowing as she did that I seldom if ever used the pool. I explained that I had done about ten laps to cool off and also to stay in shape. All the while I am sucking in my Coors belly. That's another thing. Lev wants me to lose twenty pounds over the next eight weeks. I say as much to Bunny who relays the information to our beloved cook-housekeeper Bridget O'Shaughnessy and that night for dinner I had a piece of chicken, half a tomato and a dish of non-fat yogurt. All I could think of after dinner was, only fifty-five more days to go.

# CHAPTER ONE

April 1965. It has now been six weeks since Jim McCaffrey pronounced me too sick to enjoy a cheeseburger. Breakfast is a joyless chore consisting of fat free milk and a cereal I am sure is called Cardboard Chunkies, one hundred percent fiber and zero percent taste. I wouldn't know. I have never seen the box. In fact I haven't been in a grocery store since late February. Too much temptation abounds. Potato chips. Malomars. Butter pecan ice cream. I don't want to think about it. I'm up to eight laps a day in the pool and I've lost eleven pounds. It'd be more but I have a jumbo package of Oreos secreted in my wall safe.

Today is a special day. This morning has been spent in the company of my intrepid hero, Sam August, American super agent, who bypassed the security in Sven Gunderson's lavish Colorado chalet outside of Boulder and retrieved the incriminating letters Gunderson was using to blackmail Senator Wilson Partridge, chairman of the Armed Services Committee. Now as Sam is climbing down the exterior wall to his waiting open-topped Corvette he is spotted by Gunderson's security force. He leaps the last ten feet, tucks and rolls and then leaps into the front seat and fires up the engine. He roars down the driveway, slipping past the iron gates just as they are closing and....I look at my watch. That's enough for now. I have a very important meeting to attend.

It is pushing one clock and I am sitting at a table at Musso & Frank with my agent Barry Loeb. I am going to meet someone very important. I don't know who. Barry won't tell me because he's afraid if I know who it is I won't show up. He's wrong about that. To escape Bridget's new found menus I would lunch with Nikita Khruschev and pick up the tab. I have promised Bunny I would behave myself. I lied. It was either that or hara kiri and I don't own a sword. I'm working on a cold Coors when our guest arrives at one o'clock sharp. I recognize him immediately. Simon Starbuck, independent television producer, self-assured self-promoter, and manufacturer of highly rated network garbage. He thrives on banal dialogue, insipid plots, men with bulging muscles and beautiful women wearing next to no clothing. His most successful show, "Babes of Bristol Beach" is in its sixth year and shows no signs of petering out. Three similar shows clutter up competing networks.

We shake hands all around, order drinks and settle down to a few minutes of small talk while we size each other up. I have heard persistent rumors that a couple of movie studios are interested in optioning my latest book, a best seller which introduced the reading public to my newest character, swashbuckling secret agent Sam August, who works sub rosa directly for the President of the United States. Is that why I'm here? No, it can't be. Simon Starbuck is strictly television. No, that isn't what this is about. It's something else.

We order lunch (I go for the rack of lamb with scalloped potatoes) and then we order refills on our drinks and get down to business. Simon Starbuck smiles at me broadly as he lights up a huge contraband Havana cigar.

"Mr. Bernardi, I'm here to buy Sam August and I'm not going to take no for an answer."

So much for 'something else'.

"I'm flattered, Mr. Starbuck, but Sam is not for sale," I smile politely.

"You haven't heard my offer," he says.

"I don't have to," I reply, throwing a dirty look in Barry's direction. As my agent he's supposed to protect me from things like this. He meets my look and then averts his eyes.

"Why don't you listen to what Simon has in mind, Joe? As a courtesy if nothing else," Barry says, staring at his well-manicured fingernails.

"Sure. Why not?" I say in an abundance of generosity.

"Well, here's how it shakes down, Joe. CBS has a pay-or-play with Turk Novinsky and they also owe me one more commitment. It's a slam dunk. Turk as Sam August with a 22 episode commitment to air, no pilot needed. Turk and his people are hot for the project and they are insisting on you as the show runner. Who else is more qualified to turn Sam August into a household name than his creator? I assured them that, for the amount of money I am willing to put up, this is a slam dunk deal. The network agrees. Get Bernardi, they said to me. Offer him anything."

"Intriguing," I say.

"This is a rich deal, Joe," Barry says hopefully. "No one in television has ever been offered anything like it."

"Well, then," I say. "I am not only intrigued but flattered as well. I envision only a couple of minor problems. The first is, I have never produced anything in my life and I wouldn't know where to start."

"You don't have to know anything, Joe," Starbuck says. "This is television. I'll hire the very best nonentities to do the scut work. Your chief function will be developing scripts with free lance writers, schmoozing with the network people, and keeping Turk happy. That's it."

"That's it?"

"That's it."

"I have another problem," I say.

"Shoot."

"Who the hell is Turk Novinsky?"

"He was second runner up in the World Bodybuilding Pageant last year in Brataslava. A real hunk. The gals drool for him."

"Lovely image. Does he speak English?"

"With a charming accent," Starbuck smiles.

"And can he act?"

"Last year he supported Steve Reeves in "Sand Monsters of Morocco"."

"Missed that one," I say.

"A small part but memorable," Starbuck says.

"A question,Mr. Starbuck. Did you actually read my book? Do you know who and what Sam August is?"

"I don't actually read, Joe. Haven't got the time but my people read for me."

"Well, very briefly, here's how it shakes down. Sam August is James Bond without the martinis and the sissy British accent. He is highly intelligent with brooding good looks. He quit the FBI because he was tired of all the bureaucratic shit he had to put up with. If I were to cast him, it would be close between Jim Garner and Steve McQueen and maybe a young kid you haven't heard of yet named Robert Redford. It most certainly wouldn't be some musclebound refugee from Eastern Europe who talks like Bela Lugosi."

Starbuck grins.

"Joe, Joe, I hear you but we can fix all that in dialogue. Besides, we haven't even touched on the money involved."

At that moment Barry slides me a folded piece of paper. I take it, open it and scan the contents. Starbuck is looking at me smugly, a huge grin on his face.

"Not bad, eh?" he says.

I refold the paper and slide it back to Barry.

"Tell me, Simon," I say, "how much would you say your production company is worth?"

He's taken aback by the question and at first, doesn't want to answer. Finally he comes up with a number which I am pretty sure is twice the actual value.

"A nice round figure," I say. "How about if I buy you out?"

The grin fades. The eyes narrow.

"What?" he croaks.

"I'll buy your company. I'll even throw in an extra ten percent for good will."

"What are you talking about? What's the catch?"

"No catch. I can write you a check this afternoon. Only one small provision. You are not to sell or produce any television programming to any television network now or at any time in the future. Ever. You owe the American public that much."

The puzzled look has been replaced by a nasty glare. His complexion has deepened from pink to crimson. He shifts his gaze to Barry.

"You warned me I'd be wasting my time, Loeb. I should have listened."

"Calm down, Simon," I say. "You're liable to get a heart attack."

"I don't get heart attacks, Bernardi. I give them," he growls.

He stands, tossing his napkin down onto the table. "I was told you were a smart guy, Bernardi. I may have misheard them. They may have been telling me you're a wise guy. "

With that he turns on his heel and strides toward the exit. I am not tempted to follow him. A rack of lamb is on its way. Barry Loeb cowers under my withering gaze. He apologizes. I graciously accept his apology though I don't mean a word of it. Barry has always been the watchful custodian of my career, always protective and always using excellent judgement. In this case the budget busting deal I was being offered tainted his perspective. Ten percent of the deal Starbuck offered me would have put Barry's little agency in the front ranks of the town's flesh peddlers. I know he is disappointed. I also know he is embarrassed. He doesn't usually make this kind of mistake and he knows I am furious. He would like to crawl under the table and hide. Short of that he would like to get up from the table and run, not walk, to the nearest exit. At that moment his salvation arrives in the person of Phineas Ogilvy, the entertainment columnist for the Los Angeles Times and one of my dearest friends. Overweight, foppish and flamboyant, most people assume he is homosexual. He isn't and has three ex-wives to prove it. Or is it four? I've lost track.

"Joseph, old top, how delightful to run into you like this. Do you mind if I join you? Of course, you don't. You needn't worry, I have already eaten. A delightful Cornish game hen with truffles. I will enjoy a postprandial brandy while we converse. And you don't mind, do you, Mr. Loeb? No, I thought not." He signals to our waiter, a geriatric old timer named Halliwell, and pulls up a chair.

Barry sees his chance and quickly rises from the table.

"Sorry, Joe,' he says, "I just remembered a long distance phone call that's coming in from Vienna. I'll just get out of the way so you two old friends can chat."

He smiles and hurries away before I can reply. Phineas stares after him, then orders a double brandy from Halliwell who turns and slowly shuffles off toward the bar.

"There is always a pallor about Mr. Loeb but today he seems whiter than usual," Phineas observes. "Methinks he is not in your good graces, Joseph."

"A minor disagreement. It'll pass."

"I would hardly call Simon Starbuck minor, old top. Ill-bred and repugnant, yes, but hardly minor. I was watching from my table across the way. Your conversation must have been intriguing. His exit in high dudgeon would have done Bette Davis proud."

"Phineas, if you are sniffing around for a story——"

"Dear boy, I already have the story. One of the major networks has ordered Starbuck to sign Joseph Bernardi and his adventuresome character, Sam August, to a long term arrangement and money is no object. Am I correct?"

"Reasonably so."

"My lead story for tomorrow's column," he says with a self-satisfied grin. "You never fail me, Joe. Now, what I need to know is, have you sold your soul to Mephistopheles and if so, for how much?"

"You know the answer to that," I reply. "Mr. Starbuck left the premises considerably less happy than when he came in."

"Ah, yes, my intrepid young friend. I suspected as much. And was yours a flat refusal?"

"They don't come any flatter, Phineas, and you can quote me."

At that moment Halliwell returns with my rack of lamb, hot and aromatic, a gourmet delight. Phineas looks over at it, leans in, sniffs and then smiles at Halliwell. "Make it two, my dear man, and hold the brandy for later."

It is now two-thirty. Refreshed by my delightful luncheon with Phineas, I am back at my typewriter, picking up where I left off. My protagonist, Sam August, the President's secret secret agent, is now racing down an icy mountain road in his topless Corvette being chased by two goons on the payroll of Sven Gunderson, mastermind Soviet operative whose real name ends in 'ov'. The moon is full, the air cold. Bullets whiz by Sam's head. Three hundred yards ahead is the railway depot. Off in the distance is the whistle of the 10:08 from Aspen. Aboard is his beautiful and ever faithful secretary Patsy Palmer accompanied by undercover CIA agent Binkley Shorts who is better known to the public as Raoul Meilliers, executive chef of the 5 star L'estrella Blanc on Lexington Avenue in New York City. I lean back in my chair and stare at the typewriter. I am formulating a brilliant scheme to rescue Sam from the clutches of villainy. Suddenly the phone rings. I reach for it, little knowing that my life is about to change and not for the better.

# CHAPTER TWO

The ringing of the phone has startled me. I'd rather not answer. Dorothy Parker had it right about an insistently ringing phone. What fresh hell is this? I would ignore it if I could but I know that I can't. I pick up and a familiar voice speaks my name. Suddenly the past rushes to overwhelm me. I don't remember how many times Army saved my life. Three for sure. There may have been others.

His full name is Armitage McLeod and he is known in the business as 'Anonymous Army'. A tall plumpish teddy bear of a man, always smiling, always affable, he is a script doctor and most of the time he works without credit sprucing up, or in some cases saving, shooting scripts in the middle of production. He doesn't get screen credit, the public has no idea who he is and in those rare instances when a producer actually options and produces one of his originals, the writing credit is a pseudonym. Nonetheless he is a gem known to every producer in town and while he specializes in action films, particularly westerns, he is prolific in all genres except feminine 'weepies'.

I met Army in 1958 during a very low time in my life. United Artists had hired our company to handle press and publicity for 'The Big Country', a splashy western with an all-star cast shooting in Red Rock Canyon as well as the San Joaquin Valley near the tiny town of Farmington. William Wyler was directing. Wyler and Gregory Peck were the producers. The script was the work of Robert Wilder, an excellent screenwriter and an even better novelist. He was back east working on a new book and unavailable so Army was hired to be on the set each day to handle changes. These come about when the actual location can't accommodate what's in the script or one or more of the stars thinks his or her dialogue could be 'improved' which is code for, 'Make my part bigger and better'. Thankfully there wasn't a lot of the latter. Peck, as both star and producer, was on hand to make sure that script tinkering was held to a minimum. Also the cast featured top of the line professionals like Jean Simmons, Charlton Heston, Carroll Baker and Burl Ives. It's always the second-tier wannabes that try to throw their weight around.

I was holed up in a two star hotel in Garden Acres, a one-horse town with a main street, a couple of rib joints, several saloons and not a whole lot more. A few miles away was the movie set where tenderfoot Easterner Peck was being taught the realities of ranching by foreman Chuck Heston. My personal life was a mess. My beloved Bunny Lesher was somewhere, I knew not where, and the ache in my heart was genuine.

Over the past couple of months I'd deteriorated from two cold Coors a day to a steady nighttime diet of the hard stuff, a glass in one hand and a very large torch in the other. But only at night, not during the day. Daytime was set aside for my hangovers. I couldn't dwell on Bunny during daylight hours, too much to do and too many people to deal with, but when the sun went down, that's when she reappeared in my thoughts like an unreachable wraith. I couldn't avoid her and I couldn't deal with her so I turned to Johnny Walker to help me forget her. Johnny wasn't much help.

Twice I got in bar fights with local farm boys that outweighed me by fifty pounds and twice Army pulled me out of there before

I ended up bruised and bloody in the street. Another time I was so plastered I plowed my rental car into a telephone pole on the outskirts of town. Army dragged me from the car and half carried me back to my room where he dropped me on the bed and left me to sober myself up.

Now here I am in my den and everything is frozen in place: Sam racing to the depot, the train approaching, the bad guys in pursuit. I forget them for the moment. They aren't going anywhere.

"Army. My God, I can't believe it. How are you, old buddy?" I ask, genuinely glad to hear from him.

"The truth, Joe? Lousy."

"Can't be," I say, knowing Army can sometimes be a doomsdayer. "Nobody in the business is more in demand than you."

"Work's okay, Joe. I'm tied up with Bob Aldrich on this airplane picture. No, it's uh—" A moment's silence. "Jesus, I don't even know why I made this call."

I don't like the sound of his voice. Something is really wrong. Can't be his health because I'm not a doctor and I'm positive he's not broke.

"Army, let's hear it."

"She's gone missing, Joe?"

"Who?"

"Linda."

"Linda? Linda Vasquez?"

"Yeah."

I remember Linda from the Big Country shoot. Slim, attractive, great smile, an aspiring actress no older than 21 with two lines of dialogue. Everybody loved her, most of all Army who was married to a harridan from hell. I didn't need to take Army's word for it. Audrey McLeod visited the set for two days and if she hadn't left on the third, I would have throttled her myself.

"Wait a minute, Army. You and Linda? What happened to

Audrey?"

"Nothing. I walked out on her years ago."

"And Linda?"

"That's what's so crazy, Joe. Linda disappeared without even a goodbye when 'The Big Country' wrapped and then suddenly she walked back into my life about a week ago. She knew about the movie, heard I was working script, and one evening she knocked on my hotel room door. I couldn't believe it. Seven years had passed and there she was again as if nothing had happened."

"But she's gone again."

"The day before yesterday. Sunday we'd spent the day in this little town across the border. Monday morning I left her at the hotel where we were staying and left for the set. When I got back sometime after six-thirty she was gone."

"Gone?"

"Gone. No letter. No note. And she'd left everything behind. Her clothes, her luggage, her jewelry, her medicine. Everything."

"Doesn't sound like the Linda I know."

"I know. I waited all night for her to come back and when she didn't, first thing in the morning I went to the police. Actually the county sheriff. A hulking Neanderthal named Dixon."

"And what did he say?"

"Not a hell of a lot. He asked a few questions like how long she'd gone missing and was she my wife and when he caught on that she was Hispanic and only a so-called girlfriend, he lost all interest. Said they didn't have the manpower to go looking for every runaway chiquita in Arizona. He said I was damned lucky she hadn't run off with my wallet and my car keys. Bigoted prick." There's a long silence and I think I hear a sob. "Oh, God," he says finally. "I'm sorry, Joe. This isn't fair. I shouldn't have called. I don't know what the hell I was thinking." There is an audible click. He has hung up. Reluctantly so do I.

I sit staring at the phone. I'm tempted to ask myself, what the hell was that all about but I'm not dense. It was a cry for help from someone who doesn't know which way to turn and I ache for him. I know Linda. She's a decent kid. If she'd wanted out she would have said so and, moreover, when she left she would have taken her stuff with her. No, this is something else and it feels all wrong. I want to call him back but I have no number. I don't even know exactly where he is. On the southern border somewhere. Luckily the border's only fifteen hundred miles long.

I lean back in my chair. I feel guilty about leaving Sam in a situation of dire peril but I also feel I should do something about Army though I don't know what. Finally I reach for the phone and dial the offices of Bowles & Bernardi, the highly successful management firm which still bears my name. In return I still pitch in when needed and for this I receive a decent sized check which I don't need. My partner Bertha Bowles, as promised many years ago, has made a wealthy man of me.

"Hi, Gorgeous, it's me," I say.

"Oh, you again," the sexy woman on the other end mutters. It's a game we play.

"Wanna ditch everything and run off with me to Tahiti?"

"Love to, boss, but I have pork chops in the fridge for tonight's dinner."

"Well, in that case, forget it," I say.

"Already forgotten," Glenda Mae says.

Glenda Mae Brown, a former beauty pageant queen, was my secretary and gal Friday and Best Pal for thirteen years, a rare blend of beauty and brains, and on those many occasions when despair had me in its grip, she was the one who jollied me out of it. Always cheerful, always with the right thing to say. I never could have made it without her. Now she's working for my protege, Zach Thorne, which makes him the second luckiest guy in the world.

"Shall I put him on?" she asks.

"Hell, no, I'm calling you. Need a favor."

"Only if you ask nicely."

"A director named Robert Aldrich is shooting a picture about airplanes on location somewhere. I need to know where. Pretty please, oh, gorgeous one."

"Time frame?"

"Immediate," I say. "You might start by calling—"

"I'll get back to you in ten minutes," she says and hangs up. Nine minutes later my phone rings and I pick up.

"Yuma, Arizona," she says. "The picture's called 'The Flight of the Phoenix' and the set is in the middle of the desert a few miles north of the city. Jimmy Stewart's the star and an old friend of yours is in the cast. Mr. Borgnine."

"Ernie? My God, I haven't talked to him in a couple of years."

"Anything else, boss?"

"Nope and thanks. Tell Zach hi."

I hang up, then grab my rolodex and flip through it, looking for West Coast Airlines. Twenty-five minutes later I have a reservation on the 3:10 flight to Yuma. I call Bunny at her office at the News and tell her I won't be home for dinner.

"Yuma? What's in Yuma?" she asks.

"An old friend in trouble," I tell her.

"What's her name?"

"Anonymous Army."

"The writer?"

"The same."

She knows all about Army and the way he got me through those tough times while Bunny was out of my life fighting the bottle and I was succumbing to it.

"When'll you be back?"

"Tomorrow evening at the latest."

"Have a nice trip," she says.

"Love you."

"Love you, too."

Quickly I pack my overnighter. Toilet articles plus one pair of socks, one pair of shorts, one tee shirt, a second tie, a second dress shirt and just in case, a woolen sweater. I also pack my .25 caliber Beretta, carefully wrapped in a small towel. I have a carry permit from the state of California but the law in Arizona may be different. I don't care. I'd rather fight a gun infraction in court than have to face down some crazed killer with nothing to protect me but my good looks. So far it's worked out.

The flight into Yuma's only airport, part civilian and part military, is uneventful and with my overnighter slung over my shoulder I find my way to a rental car company. The young lady at the counter is a total blank when I ask how to get to the movie location but not so a young Air Force sergeant standing nearby who knows all about it. He tells me to take 4th Avenue north toward Winterhaven. I can't miss it.

I do as I'm told and about six miles out I come across a dirt road off to the right. A makeshift barrier is in place, a uniformed security guard is sitting on a folding chair beneath an umbrella and a grey and white sedan marked 'Dempsey Security' is parked nearby. I pull up to the barrier as the rent-a-cop heaves himself up onto his feet and steps over to my late model Ford. I roll down my window.

"Restricted area, sir," he says."No admittance."

"Flight of the Phoenix?" I ask.

"You with the company?"

"Visiting a friend. Armitage McLeod. He's the writer."

"You expected?"

"It's supposed to be a surprise."

I hand the guy one of my business cards. He scopes it out, then removes his walkie-talkie from his belt and walks away, talking to someone on the set. A moment later he returns.

"Your friend's not there, sir. Sorry."

He tries to hand the card back but I don't take it.

"Tell Ernest Borgnine Joe Bernardi is here to see him."

He gives me the fisheye like I just told him LBJ was coming for dinner but he walks away. This time when he returns he's more accommodating.

"Straight down the road, sir. About a half mile. Park by the trailers. Somebody will walk you over to the set."

"Thanks," I say as he lifts the barrier to let me through.

Thirty seconds later I come up over a slight rise in the road and spot the caravan in the distance. As I get closer I count five trucks, maybe ten trailers, eight motorhomes, and a dozen cars crowded together. Close by is a huge tent and far off to the right I see what appears to be a wreck of an airplane with at least a dozen lights and reflectors aimed at it. The camera is mounted on a forklift and covered with a tarp. A dozen or so crew members are puttering around but basically the set is momentarily shut down.

A good looking young man wearing dark glasses and a panama hat directs me to a spot behind the catering truck and when I exit my car he leads me toward the oversized tent which is serving as the production center. His name is Rick Isaacs and he's a trainee assigned to the picture by the Director's Guild. Every picture gets one. His job is to open his ears, shut his mouth and sop up whatever experience he can glean. Other than that he is a glorified gofer as in, "Rick, go fer coffee for Mr. Stewart" or "Rick, go fer Mr. Kruger's script he left in his trailer."

As we get close to the tent a man with an intimidating midsection steps outside and awaits us, hands on hips and a broad grin on his face. Ernie Borgnine hasn't changed much in the ten years since we worked together on 'Marty'.

"Thank God," he says, moving to me, arms spread wide. "If

anybody can save this picture, it's you, paisan." He gives me a huge Italian embrace which I return.

"Eight years and you haven't gotten any better looking, pal," I say.

"If I got better looking, I wouldn't have a career," he laughs. "So, what's up, Joe? You didn't come all the way out here just to visit me so are you gonna handle the picture or what?"

"I'm out of that business, Ernie. No, I came down looking for Army McLeod."

His smile fades. "Come on, let's get in out of the sun."

We step into the tent which, while not cool, is better than outside. There are a half dozen tables with chairs here and there, a generator, a mimeograph machine, a short wave radio, bulletin board and other assorted essentials for a movie company on a primitive location shoot. There's also an attractive young lady, undoubtedly a production assistant, operating the mimeo and Rick Isaacs hasn't wasted a moment in volunteering to help her out. I suspect no one spends much time in here unless necessary. Those Airstream travel trailers and motor homes for the director and the cast members parked next to the equipment trucks look far more comfortable.

"About Army, Joe. He hasn't showed in a couple of days and Aldrich is on the warpath. No word, no nothin'. He just dropped out of sight."

"I talked to him early this morning, Ernie. He's a wreck. An old flame named Linda walked out on him without a word. The cops won't help and he's going nuts."

"Makes no sense, Joe. That Linda, he couldn't stop talking about her. I never met her, she never came to the set, but from what Army said about her, she wouldn't just leave like that. Gotta be something else going on."

"That's what Army thinks. It's the reason he called me. He doesn't know where to turn."

Just then the tent flap behind us opens and two tall men enter. One is lanky though not as lanky as he used to be. He's wearing a leather flight jacket and khaki trousers, his face shows a wrinkle or two and his hair is starting to grey but anyone who couldn't recognize Jimmy Stewart doesn't go to many movies. The other tall man, bearded and considerably beefier, is not familiar. He walks straight toward me.

"You the fella who came to see Army McLeod?" he asks.

I nod and put out my hand.

"Joe Bernardi."

My hand gets ignored.

"Where the hell is he?" the man says gruffly.

"I have no clue," I say, a little annoyed, "and I didn't catch your name."

"Bob Aldrich. I'm the director."

I should have known. I've never met him but his reputation precedes him. Blunt, gruff, sometimes rude, a no nonsense guy who demands a hundred percent from everyone who works for him and has apparently spent very little time honing the social graces.

"Joe talked to Army on the phone this morning, Bob," Ernie says. "Sounds like he might be in some kind of trouble. That's the reason Joe's here."

"That right, Mr. Bernardi?" Aldrich asks.

"I didn't know where he was staying. That's why I came here."

"Well, I like the guy. I hope he's okay," Aldrich says, "but right now I've got a picture to make and I can't make it without a rewrite on the next scene and since neither Jimmy nor I are writers and neither is anybody else out here at this godforsaken location, we are totally screwed."

"Well, maybe not totally, Bob," Jimmy drawls. "Mr. Bernardi here is a writer, I believe. Am I right, Joe? Wildcatters? Last year? Academy nomination?"

"Well, yes," I start to say.

"Say, that's great," Aldrich says, almost smiling. "Maybe you could help out until we can locate Army."

"Oh, I don't know—"I say, shaking my head.

"It won't take a lot of time, Joe," Jimmy says. "Just a couple of pages that need a professional touch. Shouldn't take more than an hour or two. Be a big favor if you could pitch in."

He looks at me hopefully. Aldrich looks at me hopefully. I look at Ernie who grins and shrugs and I'm thinking, what the hell am I getting myself into?

# CHAPTER THREE

It takes me a little over an hour to read the script so that I have some idea of what this film is about. Is it intriguing? You bet. Can I help? Not sure. When I am ready, we sit down at a table, the six of us, and carefully read the scene which, in Aldrich's opinion, just lays there. He and I and Stewart are joined by German actor Hardy Kruger and England's own Richard Attenborough. The sixth member of the group is that very attractive production assistant. Her name is Sherry Banks and she takes shorthand.

The plot in a nutshell. A Fairchild C-82 flying over Libya with both cargo and passengers gets caught in a sandstorm, the engines quit and the pilot (Stewart) has to crash-land. Two oil workers are killed, a third injured and while the plane has suffered damage, it's still in one piece. A cargo of dates ensures food for a considerable time but water is in short supply. The situation becomes potentially more deadly when they realize that the storm blew them considerably off course and if there is a search party, it will undoubtedly be looking in the wrong place. Kruger, playing an aeronautical engineer named Dorfmann, convinces pilot Frank Towns (Stewart), navigator Lew Moran (Atternborough) and the others that a flyable aircraft can be created from the wreckage of the C-82. Everyone pitches in following Dorfmann's instructions.

Then comes the crucial scene which, in Aldrich's opinion, 'just lays there'. Towns and Moran learn that Dorfmann is indeed an aeronautical engineer but all of his expertise is in the design and manufacture of toy airplanes.

The scene is a surprise and a shock and once revealed it needs to maintain and build tension, alleviated in spots by a little black humor. We all agree on that approach and for an hour and a half, we kick around ideas, using some, discarding others, with everyone making a contribution. At last the actors are happy. They believe they can play the scene with honesty and Aldrich is also satisfied.

Just as we are wrapping up, Rick Isaacs comes in and whispers in Aldrich's ear. He nods and Rick leaves. My watch reads quarter to seven. We all had placed dinner orders with the caterer at six when the crew sat down to eat. Our dinners will be waiting for us out by the catering truck, kept hot by warming plates. I am a tad leery of a caterer called Miguel & Luigi's and a menu which is half Italian and half Hispanic: chicken cacciatori or arroz con pollo, lasagna or burritos, gazpacho or minestrone. No fried chicken, no meatloaf and no fish and chips. Even though the arroz con pollo is lower in calories, I opted for the spaghetti and meatballs, always a safe bet when dealing with an unknown caterer. Sixteen years of eating location food has taught me many valuable lessons.

As we head out toward the catering truck, Aldrich tugs at my elbow.

"I sent one of my teamsters into town to make you a reservation at the Coronado. That's where McLeod is staying. Your room will be ready no matter how late you show up."

"Thanks," I say.

"No, Joe," Aldrich smiles. "Thank you."

We sit around over supper for about 45 minutes swapping location war stories. Aldrich proves to be a real person beneath that gruff exterior and Jimmy Stewart is exactly what you'd expect only smarter. There's a keen mind beneath all that 'Aw shucks' nonsense. Attenborough is droll, Kruger is hearty and Ernie, who waited dinner to eat with us, is Ernie. Despite the heat and the sand and the scorpions, this is not an unhappy set. At least not yet. A couple of weeks from now it may be a different story. Sherry Banks, instinctively realizing that a tableful of guys yakking about the good old days is not the best place for a 22 year old newbie, has chosen a spot across the way to eat in solitude despite our half-hearted invitation for her to join us. She isn't alone long. The slick looking DGA trainee, Rick Isaacs, has joined her for a round of outrageous flirtation and if she objects to it, she gives no sign. Location romances are a dime a dozen and invariably harmless. I hope this one is as well. Sherry seems like a nice kid.

I stick around for another hour or so as Aldrich rehearses the scene. We change a word or two, nothing major. Everyone's happy and they get ready to shoot. I head for my car after getting directions to the Coronado. It's on Fourth Avenue. I can't miss it. I've heard that before but in this case my fears were unfounded. It's pleasant looking and very welcoming. I grab my overnighter from the trunk and walk in a few minutes before ten. As promised my room is ready. I ask the clerk if Mr. McLeod is in his room. He says no, no one has seen him and his bed hasn't been slept in but he's paid up through the weekend. I write a note containing my room number and ask the clerk to stick it in Army's cubbyhole, just in case. Finally I head for the elevator and what I hope is a nice comfortable bed.

The good news is that I sleep right through to eight fifteen without interruption. The bad news is, there are no messages on my phone and when I go down for breakfast, the day clerk tells me that Mr. McLeod has not returned to his room. I ask where the Sheriff's office is located and after a quick breakfast of a bagel, juice and coffee, I drive to S. Third Avenue in search of Joshua J. Dixon who apparently is far too busy to chase after Hispanic chiquitas but might find time for a fair-skinned descendant of Scottish kings named McLeod.

The guy at the desk asks if I have an appointment and when I say no, he seems genuinely annoyed. He tells me to take a seat. Ten minutes later an olive-skinned Hispanic sergeant appears to tell me that Sheriff Dixon is in a meeting but he'll get to me as soon as possible. Many minutes pass. Shortly after ten o'clock a very attractive woman in a skimpy wardrobe and slightly smeared makeup appears from the back offices and exits the premises. A minute later the sergeant tells me that Sheriff Dixon can see me now.

Joshua Dixon is a big guy, barrel chested with a flat gut and military cut grey hair. He might be 50 years old but in a scrap with a perp half his age, I'd go with Dixon. It's not just the physique, it's something in his eyes that says 'Don't tread on me'. He doesn't bother to get up from his desk when I walk in and he doesn't waste any time on small talk.

"People who want to talk to me usually make an appointment," he says.

"Sorry. I didn't know," I say.

"What can I do for you?" he asks.

"My name is Joseph Bernardi," I say, which is as far as I get.

"That wasn't my question", he interrupts matter-of-factly staring me down.

Okay. Now that we've established who's top dog in the room, I continue.

"A friend of mine has disappeared," I say. "Armitage McLeod. He was in here the other day."

Dixon shakes his head blankly.

"He reported a woman missing. Linda Vasquez."

Now he nods.

"That guy. Now I remember. He was shacked up over at the Coronado with some little chicana. She ran out on him."

"I'm not sure that's the way it happened but, yes, that's my friend."

Dixon regards me with more a sneer than a smile.

"Tell me, Mr. uh—"

"Bernardi."

"Mr. Bernardi. Do I look like I run a lonely hearts club around here?"

"No, but—"

"Because I've got no time to chase around after your pal or his Mex girlfriend. Grown man, grown woman. What they do is their business and right now you are wasting my time."

"Both these disappearances are uncharacteristic," I say, "and it's very possible there's more here than just two missing people."

"Your opinion, not mine. Now are you going to leave or do you have to be escorted from the building?"

I make no effort to move as Dixon stares me down. I've seen guys like him before but usually they're wearing three piece suits and sitting behind big mahogany desks at sprawling movie studios. Harry Cohn and Louis B. Mayer spring to mind. They're both dead but the memory lingers on. The ego, the iron fist, the absolute control. Fuck with me at your own risk. Such is Joshua Dixon.

"The movie company just outside of town, would you say their presence is good for Yuma?" I ask.

"What kind of a question is that?"

"A simple yes or no will do," I say. "If you prefer I'll ask it of your mayor."

"Sure, it's good. We pick up a nice fee and the tourists love it when the stars come to town on the weekends. It's good for business."

"How do you think your local business people are going to feel when they learn that the film company out there in the desert is the last one that's ever going to come to Yuma to make a movie?"

"Is that right?" Dixon asks with a smile.

"Yes, that's right because I'm going to arrange it."

"Really?" Still smiling.

"Yes, really. When the studios find out that law and order in this town is subject to the caprices of a thick headed sheriff who answers to no one but his own ego, I'm sure they'll feel well rid of this place for a location, especially when Tucson or Sedona might be far more accommodating."

Dixon reddens and gets to his feet, rolling his chair backwards so that it slams against the wall. Unintimidated, I continue.

"Right now you're asking yourself, who is this asshole and what kind of bullshit is this? Well, Sheriff, I'm going to show you." I point to his phone. "Pick up the receiver, get Los Angeles information and ask to be connected to Warner Brothers Studio. When you've got a studio operator, ask for Jack Warner, the studio head, and say that Joe Bernardi is calling."

I look up at Dixon who is glaring down at me. I suspect he'd like to kick my teeth in but he knows he can't and he also can't be sure I'm bluffing. After a few seconds I get to my feet.

"Maybe I'd better take this up with the Mayor," I say and head for the door.

"What do you want?" I hear Dixon say.

I turn back to him.

"What I came in here for, Sheriff. At least a minimum effort in trying to locate my friend Mr. McLeod and the young woman Linda Vasquez. They might be in Guadalajara by now but I doubt it. Look, you can't be faulted if you come up empty but I promise you, I will make your life hell if you don't make the effort."

He hesitates, then nods.

"Give your particulars to Sergeant Ramos out at the desk. We'll do what we can."

"Thank you," I say. "I'll check back with you later this

afternoon."

"You do that," Dixon grumbles, sitting back down at his desk and dismissively starting to riff through some paperwork.

For want of something better to do, I drive out to the set. For one thing Army may have showed up though I doubt it. For another I have no clue how I would track him down on my own in this strange city in a strange state at the ass-end of the country. I'm pretty sure I have left Joshua Dixon motivated enough to give his search some real effort.

The sentry by the umbrella sees me coming, recognizes the car and raises the barrier. I wave with a smile as I speed through. As I near the set I see all kinds of activity in and around the plane wreck. Aldrich is shooting a scene and I have to assume the access road is not in the shot, otherwise the third assistant director would have been out here turning me back. Once again I pull up next to the catering truck. Miguel and Luigi and Luigi's wife Maria are clearing away the remains of breakfast and preparing for lunch. Maria is writing the menu on a blackboard and so far I see tacos, burritos, lasagna, and tortellini.

I catch Luigi's eye and ask for a mug of coffee. He's happy to oblige. He's a rotund pleasant man, always smiling, always helpful. His partner Miguel, slim and hawk-like, is less so. His wife Carlotta has been running their cantina in Yuma for the past couple of weeks though I've been told she's been spending the last few days in Tucson taking care of her sick mother.

I wander off in the direction of the set, watching warily for the camera position so I don't end up in the scene. I needn't have worried. Several of the cast members are crowded beneath one of the wings apparently arguing among themselves. I recognize Dan Duryea and George Kennedy and a couple of British actors whose names escape me. I walk up to the sound man and park behind him. I spot Ernie watching and wave. He waves back.

Something catches my eye as I look out past the wounded plane to the desert beyond. Two men aboard a jeep are approaching at mach speed. They fly by and skid to a halt next to the production tent. One man ducks inside, the other jogs toward the cluster of trucks and trailers. A few moments later he hurries back accompanied by Miguel Moreno, the caterer. The other man emerges from the production tent with Sherry Banks and the location nurse at his side. Sherry hurries toward the set while the others climb aboard the jeep which races back the way it came.

Aldrich has just cut the scene as Sherry threads her way toward Cliff Coleman, the assistant director. She whispers in Coleman's ear and Coleman immediately goes to Aldrich who listens and then wraps the set. Everyone starts gabbing at once, trying to figure what happened. Ernie's been talking to the second a.d. I grab him.

"What's going on?" I ask him.

"Sounds like the scout party found a dead body out there in the dunes about a quarter of a mile from here?" Ernie says.

"Somebody from the company?"

"Not sure. They're radioing for an ambulance and notifying the Sheriff's department." He falls silent for a moment. "I heard someone say it might be Miguel Moreno's wife Carlotta."

"Isn't she supposed to be in Tucson taking care of her mother?"

"Yeah. Supposed to be," Ernie says flatly.

Nineteen minutes later the ambulance comes wailing up to the production tent followed by the Sheriff's department's Jeep Wagoneer. Sergeant Ramos and two deputies get out and along with the ambulance personnel start querying the scout team. A lot of jabbering, a lot of pointing. A moment later the medical team climbs aboard a jeep and heads out for the dunes. Ramos and his men follow in the four wheel drive Wagoneer. Miguel goes with them. Bad news for Miguel, I think. The cumbersome ambulance, ill equipped for the soft desert sand, stays put.

Everyone is standing around in little clusters, talking and wondering. The minutes drag by though speculation runs rampant. What was Carlotta doing out in the desert? When did she get back from Tucson? Maybe she never went to Tucson at all. Maybe she and Miguel were having problems? How did she die? Accidentally or was it something else?

Finally in the distance I spot a cloud of dust. They are returning. I amble over toward the ambulance as the vehicles come to a stop. Miguel emerges from the Sheriff's vehicle, visibly shaken, his face drawn. The medical people open the rear door of the ambulance, then hurry to the back of the Wagoneer and lift out the body which is lying on a stretcher. Muted voices can be heard as the woman's body is carried to the back of the ambulance. I hear Carlotta's name being spoken in hushed terms but no one is crying. This is a male cast and a male crew. Tears are withheld even though feelings may run deep.

I am tall but nonetheless I stand on tiptoe for a better look as the body is loaded into the ambulance.

A chill rattles my body. A night among the animals on the desert floor cannot be good for a corpse. Still, she is recognizable. The others may be mourning the death of Carlotta Moreno. I am not. The Sheriff and his people have made good. They have found Linda Vasquez.

# CHAPTER FOUR

The ambulance has just left with Miguel Moreno aboard, headed for Parkview Hospital which houses the local morgue. It will be met by the county medical examiner and sometime this afternoon an autopsy will be performed. For obvious reasons Aldrich has wrapped for the day and cast and crew are scattering, most headed for Yuma where they are billeted at various motels around town. Aldrich and the actors are all staying at the Coronado which boasts the city's most upscale accommodations. A few minutes ago Sergeant Ramos radioed headquarters for a forensics team to comb the scene of the crime for clues and they should be arriving shortly but by late this afternoon, no one will be left on this site except the security force. Ernie has asked me to join him for lunch but I begged off with the excuse that I had just eaten a hearty breakfast. A lie but I need to tarry. I want a few minutes with Luigi Vecchio and his wife Maria. As the yellow bus prepares to leave with most of the crew and the private cars hasten toward the main road into town, I wander in the direction of the catering truck.

Maria Vecchio is erasing the menu board. The goodies will have to wait until tomorrow. She is relatively attractive, matronly but with a warm smile and everyone seems to like her. I know I do.

She looks up.

"We're just closing up, Mr. Bernardi, but if you're hungry I could fix you something."

"Thanks, Maria, but I'm fine," I say. "Just checking to see how you and Luigi are getting along. This must have come as a shock to you both."

"Yes, very much so. And poor Miguel. Did you see him? My heart breaks for him."

I nod.

"The shock of it must have been awful." I say. "One moment he believes his wife is safely in Tucson visiting a sick mother, the next he's staring into her cold dead face. I don't know how he was able to handle it."

"Faith, Mr. Bernardi," Luigi says as he steps out of the truck. He's carrying a couple of uncapped bottles of Dos Equis. He hands me one. "A strong faith in God's will, even when it is beyond comprehension."

We clink bottles and drink. Luigi believes in God. Despite my doctors, I believe in beer.

"So, how long were they married?" I ask.

Luigi shoots Maria a quick look.

"Not every marriage requires a document," she says.

I nod.

"I understand," I say. "Then how long were they together?"

"Three years," Luigi says. "I remember the day Carlotta came to the back door of our cantina offering to work for a meal. She was thin then. How you say, scrawny, and not so beautiful. Miguel brought her in and fed her leftovers we would have thrown away. You could see she hadn't eaten in couple of days but she was very nice, very grateful. Maria and I we had a spare bedroom. We took her home with us and the next day we put her to work washing dishes and clearing tables. After a couple of days we made her a waitress. Her Spanish was perfect and the customers liked her. After a week she started going home after work with Miguel."

"They must have been very much in love," I say.

Maria smiles.

"Perhaps so, but in the beginning she was frightened and homeless and needed protection and he was a man with a man's needs. A good arrangement, but yes, this past year, I think perhaps there was love between them."

"Did she ever talk about her past? Where she came from?"

Luigi regards me curiously.

"You ask a lot of questions, Mr. Bernardi."

I shrug.

"I'm a writer. I find their situation fascinating. Someday I might write about it, changing the names, of course."

"Yes, I understand," Luigi smiles. "And you are right. Like something you see in the movies. Richard Burton and Elizabeth Taylor, yes?"

"Not sure I'd go that far," I say.

I sit back and enjoy my beer as Luigi and Maria, no longer suspicious of my curiosity, tell me all I need to know about Carlotta nee Linda Vasquez. Remembering Linda as she had been seven years ago, it was not easy to listen to. Vague about her early years she'd talked about trying to make it as an actress, then slipping downward month by month. Working as a B-girl in dives in Los Angeles and Anaheim and San Diego, getting high on marijuana and then hooked on heroin, picked up by the police and sent to a hospital for treatment and after nine weeks of drying out, escaping and making her way to Yuma, determined to stay clean no matter what it took.

"And that she did," Luigi says. "If she was using, I saw no sign of it. She had become one of us and she was trusted. Once or twice a week she would drive our panel truck into San Luisina across the border to pick up beer from the distributor and produce from the farmer's market. She was a loved person, Mr. Bernardi, by Maria and me and by Miguel and our customers. All who knew her loved her and that is why I cannot understand this terrible thing that has happened."

"I can't either, Luigi," I say, "but I am going to find out."

I'm back at the Coronado by two-thirty and no, there is no sign of Army. I go to my room and call Glenda Mae. I need more help. I ask her to check with the Writer's Guild for the name of Army's agent as well as an address and/or a phone number for his wife Audrey. Even though they have been separated for years I'm pretty positive she's still listed as beneficiary on his pension plan insurance benefit. He'd make sure his two kids weren't abandoned if he should unexpectedly keel over.

His agent is a guy named Philby with Ashley-Famous. I call and finally get him on the line, probably after somebody let him know who I am. He's all caramel and whipped cream and after hanging on a dead phone line for seven minutes I am not. I ask if he's heard from Army. He is blank until I remind Philby that he represents him. He finally dials in and says he hasn't heard from Army since he made the deal with 20th for the airplane picture. I hang up with a curt goodbye and dial Audrey McLeod who is now living in Sacramento. When I give my name, she hangs up on me. I redial.

"I hope this isn't Bernardi again," she says, picking up.

"It is and you can either talk to me or talk to the police."

"Yeah? What about?"

"Army."

"Is he dead? Please, tell me he's dead."

"No such luck, Audrey, but he is missing. I'm calling to find out if you know where he is."

"Fat chance," she says.

"Or where he might have disappeared to. An old friend, maybe."

"Except for a check I receive every month from his bank, I've had nothing to do with the son of a bitch for almost eight years. So, no, I do not know where he is or where he might be and if you find out he's croaked, please call me as I understand from the Writers Guild he is worth twenty thousand dollars to me in a pine box."

Click. She's gone. I know there must have been a good reason why Army married this woman many years ago but none comes quickly to mind.

Now I call Bunny at her desk at the News where I have a reasonable expectation of some love and respect. I am not disappointed. She has missed me and has worried about me. I tell her I'm fine which pleases her and then I tell her that Army has disappeared. This does not please her because she knows that now I will go out and try to find him. Sometimes having a wife who can read your mind, even when several hundred miles away, can be a major annoyance.

I kill a couple of hours reading the local paper and half-watching some inane game show but by four-thirty I'm out of patience. Surely Sheriff Dixon must know something by now. Whether he'll share it is a whole other matter.

The same desk sergeant gives me the same runaround I got earlier. No appointment? Take a seat. A few minutes go by. Sergeant Ramos appears. No word yet on your friends. Go back to your hotel. Call us tomorrow. I tell Ramos I have vital information on the murder at the movie location. Tell me, Ramos says. I'll tell Dixon, I say.

A few minutes later Dixon leans forward at his desk and fixes me with an icy stare. "Okay," he says. "Let's have it."

"You first," I reply.

"Come again?"

"I said, you first. The only way I can get any cooperation out of you is to bludgeon you with hard ball. So tell me about the police report."

"Confidential."

"My lips are sealed."

"Now what have you got for me?"

"I just told you, my lips are sealed."

Dixon sighs in frustration.

"You know I could have you locked up for obstruction," he says.

"Lead the way," I say. "Almost suppertime and I could use a free meal."

I stare at him. He stares at me. Finally he picks up a file folder on his desk and shoves it in my direction. I pick it up. The police report. I scan the salient points.

"Single shot, back of the head. .25 caliber," I say.

"That's right."

"Mob hit," I say.

"Seems that way."

"I didn't know Yuma had a mob problem."

"Neither did I," Dixon responds.

"Cigarette burns?" I comment as I continue to scan the pages.

"Dozens of them," Dixon says. "All over her body. She went through hell. Somebody wanted something from her, God knows what. Whether they got it, who knows."

"Time of death? Yeah, here it is," I say. "No more than two days ago. Lividity shows body died elsewhere and was moved to the desert." I look up at Dixon. "Somebody wanted the movie company to find her. Why?"

"You tell me. You know, Bernardi, you think and talk an awful lot like a cop."

"I have friends who teach me well."

"And now you have something for me."

"You know that missing woman I wanted you to find for me? Linda Vasquez? She's your d.b."

"No. Carlotta Moreno."

"Carlotta Moreno and Linda Vasquez. One and the same. She's

Mrs. Carlotta Moreno here in Yuma even though she isn't actually married to Miguel Moreno but before she arrived here, she was Linda Vasquez. Both Armitage McLeod and I knew her seven years ago when she was a bit part actress on a movie called 'The Big Country'."

"You're positive?"

"Positive."

"And your friend McLeod is missing."

"Yes."

"Where is he, Mr. Bernardi?"

"I don't know."

"I was serious about that obstruction charge."

"I'm sure you were but I still don't know where he is. Maybe he's dead, too."

"Maybe. And maybe your friend killed the lady and ran for it."

"Maybe. But I doubt it."

"You have anything else for me?" Dixon asks.

"No. That's it. I'll check back with you tomorrow."

"I can't wait," Dixon says, leaning back in his chair.

I'm back at the Coronado by five-thirty and very hungry. It's early for supper but I realize I had no lunch. From the entrance I peer into the dining room hoping to see a familiar face. I hate eating alone in public. It stamps you as a loser. No luck. The place is virtually empty except for a table in the rear where Miguel Moreno is eating. Or at least he's trying to. Standing across from him is the DGA trainee, Rick Isaacs, who is animated while Moreno is doing his best to ignore him. Finally Isaacs turns away and strides toward me, his face grim. As he gets close and recognizes me, his sunny self-effacing smile breaks out and he greets me warmly as he walks past me. I watch him go and wonder which of the two Rick Isaacs I just saw is the real one. I wonder if Sherry Banks knows.

I debate sitting down with Moreno and decide not to. Maybe he knows about Linda Vasquez, maybe he doesn't, but I think that's something I will keep between the sheriff and me for the time being. In any case, if I am going to pump him, I'm going to do so when we don't run the risk of constant interruption by sympathizers and well-wishers.

I walk over to the front desk to check for messages and see immediately that Army's cubbyhole is empty.

"What happened to those messages for 122?" I ask.

"In the trash, Mr. Bernardi. Mr. McLeod called in shortly after lunch and I read them to him."

"You're sure it was Mr. McLeod?"

"Oh, yes, I recognized his voice."

"Did he say where he was calling from?"

"I didn't ask him that. I just relayed the messages," the clerk says.

I nod and head for the elevator. The good news is, Army is alive. That is, if it really was Army who called. I'm beginning to like this situation less and less and the possible involvement of organized crime is not helping. I try to picture a fuzz ball like Army involved with the mob. I can't.

Once in my room, I order a cheeseburger and coffee from room service. I'm told there will be a thirty minute wait. I dig into the snack bar for a bag of chips to tide me over and flip on the evening news. Predictably it's all bad. Students are violently protesting the Viet Nam war and Negroes are non-violently protesting segregation. Or at least that's the idea. White Southern sheriffs have other ideas. The phone rings and I turn off the bad news.

"Yeah?"

"Joe?"

"Army?"

"Yeah."

"Where are you?"

"Here."

"Where's here?"

"In town."

"We have to talk. Come to the hotel."

"No!" he says fearfully. "I can't. Too dangerous."

"All right," I say. "I'll come to you."

There's a long silence.

"All right, but be careful. Make sure you're not followed."

He gives me an address on 23rd Street and simple directions.

"It's a private house. I'm renting a room. Ask for Steve Leech."

I laugh out loud. Steve Leech is the name of the character played by Chuck Heston in 'The Big Country'.

"I'm leaving now. See you in a few."

I hang up and grab my car keys. Just as I reach the door, there's a knock. I open it and the room service waiter is standing there with my supper on a tray. I slip him a buck.

"Stick it on the table and leave the lid on," I tell him and then I hurry down the corridor toward the elevator.

# CHAPTER FIVE

I find the house with ease. It's a one-story ranch sitting close to the sidewalk in a middle class neighborhood. I park on the street and walk up the driveway to the slate walkway leading to the front door. I knock and a moment later, a grey-haired woman opens the door a few inches and peers out at me suspiciously. I toss her my most winning smile.

"I'm here to see Steve Leech," I say.

"In the back," she says brusquely, swinging the door open. I step inside. The place is a lot smaller than it looks from the street and there's an odor I don't really recognize. Must, maybe. Or mold. The living room's not very tidy and the television is tuned to a wrestling match. Sitting in an easy chair eating from an aluminum tray is an obese teenager wearing a Hawaiian shirt and shorts. A TV tray and dinner is set up in front of the other easy chair in the room. The old lady points toward the rear of the house.

"Take a right at the end of the hallway. First door on your left."

She plunks herself down in front of her dinner as a blonde hulk in braids hits the ring floor with a thud and a bald hulk jumps on top of him, kneeing him in the groin. If I didn't know better I'd say one or both of these gentlemen will end up in a hospital before midnight. But since I do know better, my judgement tells me they'll be knocking back tequila shots together at some local saloon around ten. I slink down the hallway and then knock softly on the door. No answer. I knock again.

"Identify yourself," comes a voice from within.

"Jim McKay, asshole," I say. "Open up." McKay is the character played by Greg Peck opposite Heston in 'The Big Country'.

The door opens a crack and a blackened eye peers out at me, then the door swings open and Army, wearing only a tank top and khaki shorts, reaches for me unsteadily.

"Joe, thank God," he says. I grab him and help him back into the room, shutting the door behind me. Army is a mess. In addition to the black eye he has a cut over his other eye, a huge purple and yellow bruise on the right side of his face and several more on his neck and shoulders. He slumps down into a chair and whatever happened I can tell he is still in pain.

"Jesus, Army, what the hell happened to you?" I ask.

He merely shakes his head as he takes three aspirin from a bottle on the table next to the chair and downs them with two hefty swallows of water.

"Joe, I'm sorry, I really am. I shouldn't have called you. You shouldn't be mixed up in this."

"What exactly is 'this'?"

"Damned if I know," he says. "All I know is Linda suddenly pops up in my life again. For the past five or six years I've just been going through the motions and then suddenly, there she is and I'm like a kid again. Almost like she'd never left. She said she'd had a few tough years but she was over it and ready to start a new life and what she meant, Joe, was a new life for the two of us. Can you imagine. Joe? After seven years, a new life. Just like that."

"Unbelievable," I say, knowing that some time in the next few minutes I am going to have to tell him something that will shatter his newfound dream.

"She wanted us to run away. The two of us. Right away. I told her I couldn't, not for a few weeks while the picture was shooting. If I walked out I'd never work on another movie. Anyway, I said I also couldn't do it because it was a commitment I had to honor. I told her I'm a man of my word. She said she understood. She said she had a way to make a lot of money for us and when she did she would go on ahead and leave me instructions on how to catch up with her. I told her no, I didn't care about a lot of money, just her, and she should stick around until the movie wrapped and then we'd take off and she said okay to that but of course, she didn't mean it because a couple of days later she disappeared. The following day there was a letter in my key box. It had been mailed the day before in Yuma. In the envelope was a note."

"Have you got the note?"

"Sure," he says. He pulls his wallet from his back pocket and extracts a small folded piece of paper. I check it out. It reads: 'Rhonda 619-887-9060. Call Thursday.' Tomorrow is Thursday.

"And you don't know what this is about."

"No," Army says.

I wave my hand at his injuries.

"And this, what's this all about?"

"I told you, I went to the Sheriff's office. No damned help there. Then I called you which I never should have done—"

"Forget that, Army. I'm here and I'm glad I am. I owe you a lot."

"No, not this."

"Yes, this. Now keep talking. You called me. Then what?"

"That evening I walked a couple of blocks to this restaurant we'd eaten at two nights in a row figuring maybe she'd show up there and when I'm inside two guys walk up behind me and one guy shows me a gun and tells me to keep walking to the back, to the kitchen and then out the back door into an alley behind the restaurant and then the guy with the gun asks me, where is it? And

I don't know what he's talking about so he slugs me with the pistol barrel across the side of my face and then holds the gun on me while the other guy starts beating the shit out of me. All the time, he keeps saying where is it? Give it up or we'll kill you. Stuff like that. Then the guy with the gun says he'll go get the car and he goes off and I'm beat to shit, laying against some garbage cans and my hand is in one of them and I can feel this bottle, heavy like a liquor bottle and when the guy who's been beating on me looks away for a second, I grab that bottle by the neck and I swing it as hard as I can at his head and he goes down and he stays down and I swear to God, Joe, I thought I might have killed him and I didn't care. I just started to run and I ran and ran, down alleys, across streets, staying to the shadows."

"And they were chasing you?"

"I don't know. I guess so. I didn't really look. And then I was in this neighborhood and I spotted this sign on a lawn. Room to rent. Weekly. This place, Joe, and I went to the door and Mrs. Beardsley opens it and I tell her I want the room and I guess she wasn't too sure about that, I mean, the way I looked, all beat up, but she says come in and she shows me the room and I am so goddamned grateful to be safe I take it right away. Eight bucks a day. Fifty-six bucks for a week. I'm lucky. I've got cash on me and I give her the fifty-six bucks and tell her tomorrow I'll go pick up my things which, of course, I don't do because I'm scared shitless of being spotted by those two goons. Yesterday I washed out my socks and underwear and dried 'em by the open window but, Jesus, Joe, I can't stay here forever."

"And these two guys, you have no idea what they wanted from you," I say.

"Not a clue." He shakes his head in frustration. "Oh, God, Joe, Linda gone, two guys trying to kill me, Aldrich must be busting a gut wondering where I went, 20th will have me blackballed by every studio in town—"

"Look," I say, "we have to get you out of here, back to the set. You'll explain to Aldrich. He's really not a bad guy and I'll back you up and—"

There's a sharp rap on the door. Army looks up, annoyed.

"Not now!" he shouts.

A voice comes from the other side of the door."

"Open up, Mr. Bernardi. We know you're in there."

Army and I share a look, then I walk to the door.

"No, Joe!" Army says.

He's afraid of goons but I recognize the voice. I open the door and Sergeant Ramos steps inside the room accompanied by one of his deputies.

"You followed me," I say.

"I thought it was a good idea." He looks over at Army. "You need to come with us, Mr. McLeod."

"Why? I haven't done anything."

"We need to ask you some questions. You, too, Bernardi."

"Questions about what?" Army says.

"The death of Carlotta Moreno."

"Why? I mean, I heard it on the radio but I've been in this room for three straight days. I never met the woman and I sure don't know anything about her death."

Ramos shrugs.

"And I suppose you didn't know that Carlotta Moreno's real name was Linda Vasquez."

Army whips his head toward me, eyes wide with shock.

"Joe!" he croaks.

We get him out of the house easily. He is in a daze, still not quite comprehending. Mrs. Beardsley is sorry to see him go but happy that she can keep all of the first week's rent. Her grandson remains parked in front of the TV set scarfing down pie and ice cream. If he's aware that we are leaving he gives no sign. The bald guy is now out of the ring and Blonde Braids is pummeling him with a cardboard sign.

Dixon was home having a late dinner, maybe alone, maybe not, so he takes his own sweet time about returning to headquarters. My watch reads 8:45 when he walks in the door. Army and I are sitting on a hard wooden bench in the reception area. Ramos' deputy is seated across from us, I think half hoping we'll try to make a break for it. Maybe it's that droopy mustache that makes him look like Pancho Villa on a bad day.

"Bring 'em in," Dixon says as he walks by us and heads for his office.

I can tell from the start this is not going to be a fun get-together.

"The dead woman," he says. "Your amigo here says she is this Linda Vasquez you wanted us to find. Would you like to see the body or will you take his word for it?"

Army just waves his hand, staring at the floor.

"Two days ago," Dixon says. "Account for your movements."

"I was staying in a room I had rented in a house on West 23rd Street."

"All day?"

"All day."

"Witnesses?"

"Mrs. Beardsley, the landlady, and her grandson."

"You're saying you never left your room and they never left the house, is that right?" Dixon asks.

"Not exactly," Army says.

"Explain not exactly."

"The kid goes to school and right before lunch, Mrs. Beardsley walked to the local grocer to do some shopping."

"How long was she gone?"

"An hour maybe."

"So for this hour you were alone in the house."

"I suppose."

"You suppose? You either were or you weren't. Or maybe you left the house and returned and neither the woman nor her grandson were aware you'd left the premises."

"I never left the premises."

"Where's your car?"

"At the Coronado."

"That'll be easy enough to check."

"Then check it!" Army snaps. Usually docile, he's getting mighty peevish as he stares at Dixon coldly.

"You have a perfectly good paid up room at the Coronado. Why did you suddenly decide to take a room in this woman's home?"

"If you really want to know, I'll tell you, Sheriff," Army says, "but if you're going to assume I'm lying, why don't we save time by skipping to another subject." Not only peevish but bitterly sarcastic.

"Let's hear it," Dixon says.

And so Army goes through his story again, the two men, the beating, the escape, the frantic racing from street to street looking for safe haven and finally finding it. Throughout Dixon has leaned back in his chair and listened intently.

"These two men," he says when Army is finished, "would you recognize them if you saw them again?"

"Yes."

Dixon leans forward on his desk.

"Allright, Mr. McLeod, I'm going to keep you here overnight. We'll call it protective custody for the moment and it's possible you'll be safer here than anywhere else. In the morning we'll go through some of my favorite photo albums. In the meantime, I would think about retaining a lawyer just to be on the safe side." He turns his head and looks at me. "Now, Mr. Bernardi, what about you?"

"What about me, Sheriff?"

"Where were you two days ago?"

"I caught the 3:10 flight to Yuma from Los Angeles, arrived about an hour later, went straight to the movie set out in the desert, helped out with the script as a favor to the director, ate dinner and at ten o'clock checked into my room at the Coronado. I hopped into bed and was asleep by ten-fifteen."

"Okay, you can leave but don't go anywhere without checking with me first."

"Just a thought, Sheriff, but three nights ago, might be helpful to check the local hospitals and ask if they had a drop-in with a possible skull fracture from an empty whiskey bottle."

"I just said you can go, Mr. Bernardi. I suggest you take advantage of this one-time opportunity. Now."

I look over at Army.

"I'll be fine," he says.

"I'll see about that lawyer," I tell him.

It's past eleven o'clock when I get back to the Coronado. I'm tired, hungry and miserable when I walk into my room and my mood brightens only slightly when I see that my cheeseburger and coffee are waiting for me on the table. A cold cheeseburger is not my idea of gourmet dining but hunger pangs are something I do not easily abide. I tear into it, sipping cold coffee between bites.

I think about calling my friend Ray Giordano, L.A.'s top criminal defense lawyer, and asking him for a recommendation, if he has one, from among Yuma's limited slate of attorneys. But no, at this hour, he's either frolicking under the sheets with his wife Trudy or watching Johnny Carson and in either case, my call will not be welcome. I strip down to my skivvies and slip into bed. Screw the world until tomorrow morning.

# CHAPTER SIX

I sleep until eight-thirty because there is no good reason I should awaken any earlier. I call room service for a carafe of coffee, orange juice and a bear claw and then I phone Ray Giordano at his office. He's an early bird who functions well before lunch, not so much afterwards. I tell him Army's story and he asks for a few minutes. My breakfast arrives. I nibble at it and then the phone rings. Ray has found someone. Her name is Angelique Garcia and she's a former prosecutor from Phoenix who got tired of big city wheeling and dealing and settled in Yuma as a defense attorney to retain her sanity. Ray gives her five stars and promises to phone her right away and pave the way for my call. I thank him for her number and settle back, contemplating my next move.

It keeps coming back to 'Rhonda 619-887-9060. Call Thursday." I have no idea what this cryptic note means but I'll never find out until I hook up with Rhonda. I pick up the phone and dial. It rings three times and then a man's recorded voice comes on the line.

"You have reached the Red Sombrero located at 901 Market Street in downtown San Diego. We open at 4:00 for Happy Hour. Dinner is served from six o'clock until ten. The lounge opens at eight o'clock with entertainment by the Chico Ramirez Quartet. Dinner reservations not required but recommended. To leave a message wait for the beep and thank you for choosing the Red Sombrero."

I hear the beep, hesitate momentarily, then hang up. I'm beginning to think the best way to approach Rhonda would be eyeball to eyeball. As I recall, San Diego isn't that far. Maybe two and a half hours by car. Absent any other brilliant ideas, it seems worth the trip.

I check my watch. Nine-thirty. It's early but I'll give her a try. I reach for the phone.

"Garcia Law Offices. How may I help you?"

A pleasant female voice. Good start.

"Ms. Garcia,please. Joseph Bernardi calling."

"This is Angelique Garcia and I've been expecting your call, Mr. Bernardi."

"Oh, I thought—"

"My gal Friday Myrna had to fly to Phoenix on personal business, hence I am answering my own phone. Ray tells me you have a major problem."

"Not me, a friend, and yes, it's major."

"Look, I'm due at the courthouse at ten-thirty. Why don't you meet me there and we can chat before my meeting?"

"Not a problem."

"I'm wearing a baby blue suit and if you don't look too closely, I bear a slight resemblance to Ava Gardner. You do know who Ava Gardner is."

"Actually I dated her once, just after she dumped Artie Shaw. I'll find you."

I go to the closet and take down my overnighter from the shelf. I remove the Beretta from its towel wrapping and slip it into my trouser pocket. It's not that I expect a shootout with Angelique Garcia but Army's situation is beginning to weigh heavily on me. Worse, I am without the proverbial scorecard without which you cannot tell the players. Better cautious than a corpse.

The courthouse is easy to find and so is Angelique and you don't have to squint to know there is a lot of Ava Gardner in that five-seven frame of hers.

She smiles and extends her hand.

"Nice to meet you, Mr. Bernardi."

"Likewise, Ms. Garcia."

"That's Miss and I prefer Angelique, Joe, if that's okay."

"Fine by me."

She suggests a cup of coffee at a small table next to the refreshment stand and when we're settled in, she asks me to fill her in on Army's predicament. I do and she listens intently.

"I'd heard about the discovery of the woman's body out on the desert," she says, "but did not know the cause of death. A small caliber bullet to the back of her head is troubling."

"You and Sheriff Dixon agree on that. Organized crime is not on his radar."

"Nor mine," she says, "and I am going to assume that Mr. McLeod is not a part of that branch of society."

"Army McLeod is a big teddy bear whose idea of high crime is a parking ticket."

"Good to hear. Unlike a lot of defense attorneys I'm choosy about who I represent. Not great for the company bank balance which is why I charge outrageously for the cases I do take on."

"He can afford it."

"Also good to hear. I assume Sheriff Dixon has him looking at mug shots."

"He said he was going to."

"Okay," she says. "Holding him last night was a good precaution but he can't stay there forever. From what you told me, I hear nothing that ties the woman's death to Mr. McLeod other than the fact that he knew her from years back under a different name." She checks her watch. "I have a meeting in judge's chambers in six minutes on another matter and then I'll drop by the Sheriff's office. Does he know about me?"

"Not yet."

"You might want to tell him. Where can I reach you?"

"I'm staying at the Coronado but I'll be gone most of the day on other business."

"All right. If you're not in, I'll leave a message." She gets up, puts out her hand and we shake. "Nice meeting you, Joe, and, by the way, I enjoyed reading both your books." She winks and with that she walks off, stiffing me with an 80 cent coffee tab. I don't mind. Watching her walk away is intriguing. Bunny would not approve.

I drive to Dixon's headquarters and as promised he has Army looking at mug shots. So far he's come up dry. I tell him about Angelique. He's excited and grateful. Dixon nods approval. As usual, Ray has come through for me. My next stop is the movie location in the desert north of town.

Things are back to normal. Shooting has resumed. Some of the actors have stripped to their trousers as they perform manual labor trying to rearrange the damaged plane into something that will fly. Reflectors are being used to intensify the light and make it seem hotter than it is- and it is hot. Sweaty torsos attest to that. They're between takes so I walk over to the plane and interrupt Aldrich who is conferring with Coleman, his assistant director. He's delighted to hear that Army has been located, less thrilled with the circumstances. I tell him it's possible that Army could be back to work as early as this afternoon but suggest that given what he's been through, additional security is probably a good idea. Aldrich agrees and Coleman says he'll see to it.

With nothing else to attend to, I drive to an on-ramp for Interstate 80 and head west to San Diego. It's about one-thirty. With luck I'll be there by four o'clock. My mind wanders as I think about Army and Linda and the shit that was dumped on them by a so-called benevolent God. In the movie the C-82 is renamed 'Phoenix' after the mystical bird that was consumed by fire and then rose again from its own ashes. Unlike the Phoenix, Linda Vasquez was flesh and blood and she won't be rising again from anywhere. Ashes to ashes, dust to dust. Once a young and beautiful woman, cut down in the prime of life, her demise is permanent. And Army, he, too, is a victim. Even if he survives this situation, his life will never be the same. Thanks, God. A job well done.

I miss my e.t.a. by twenty minutes due to road construction just east of Bostonia. It's four-thirty when I pull into a parking lot on Market Street, a block away from the Red Sombrero. I walk back along the sidewalk and take a closer look. I'm not surprised by what I see. It's small and ratty, a dive with a capital D. Luigi and Maria had told me Linda had gone through hell. The Red Sombrero was obviously part of that old neighborhood.

I walk in. The foyer is dimly lit. Off to my left is the bar and to my right is a lounge with lots of tiny round tables and a miniscule bandstand. Straight ahead is another room which I can't see into but there's a podium by the entrance with a sign "Please Wait to Be Seated." It's possible the Board of Health knows about this place but I wouldn't put money on it. I step into the bar and pull up a stool. The crowds have yet to appear. An old man is wiping off the tables and filling the peanut bowls and a floozy with a bad dye job is sitting at the end of the bar nursing something tall. Other than that, I'm it. A small sign on the mirror reads "Happy Hour- 4 to 6." Nobody here is happy and that includes the bartender who gives me a fishy look before he walks over to me. Probably my shirt and tie. Or the fact that I shaved this morning. One thing he's sure of. I'm not a regular.

"What'll it be?"

"Stoli on the rocks with a twist." I say. I don't really want it but bartenders tend to be more forthcoming with information if you spend a few bucks and seltzer water with a lime isn't going to do it. He brings my drink. I down half of it, indicating I am a hopeless lush, and drop a twenty on the bar.

"Rhonda around?" I ask casually.

"You a friend of hers?" the barkeep asks.

"You bet."

"If you're a friend you'd know she doesn't get here until eight." I nod.

"She live around here?"

"I wouldn't know. Why don't you come back at eight and give your name to security. Leo is very accommodating. Maybe he can help you." He smiles and I spot a glob of spinach between two of his front teeth.

I give the guy a big smile in return and pick up my twenty, then lay down three ones. I get up from the stool and head for the doorway.

"You got a dime coming," he calls after me.

"Buy yourself a toothbrush," I say.

In the foyer I start toward the front entrance. The peanut guy who slipped out when I wasn't looking grabs my arm.

"You looking for Rhonda?" he asks.

"You know where I can find her?"

"You still hanging on to that twenty?"

I reach in my pocket and hold it up so he gets a good look at it.

"Halfway down the block. A crummy apartment house. 885 Market. Second floor. 2D. If she's not there, try the bar on the corner. The lady is very partial to scotch neat with water back and the time of day is immaterial."

I nod. He snatches the bill and I step out the door onto Market Street, check the numbers and start walking west. Mr. Peanut was right. The place is crummy, all right, right down to the crumbling front stoop and the cracked window on a first floor unit. If it was a patient, this dump would be be on life support. I walk into the vestibule, avoiding a single roller skate on the linoleum floor and check the mail boxes. 2D belongs to R. Scanlan. I climb the stairs. I'm tempted to say the place needs a paint job but I suspect it just had one twenty years ago. I walk down the second floor corridor inhaling the aroma of fried onions, a hint of body odor and perhaps a trace of urine. I knock softly on the door to 2D. A female voice from within calls out "Yeah??" I knock again and a moment later the door opens.

Rhonda Scanlan is a relatively attractive woman on the wrong side of thirty and what she had at 21 she no longer has. She's wearing a terry cloth robe and instinct tells me that's all she's wearing. She glares at me defiantly.

"What do you want?" she asks.

"Conversation."

"Find yourself a shrink," she says, the aroma of Jim Beam wafting in my direction. She starts to close the door.

"I'm Army McLeod," I say.

Her eyes widen and the blood drains from her face.

"Oh, my God," she says and quickly juts her head out into the hallway, looking in both directions. She grabs me by my tie and yanks me into her apartment, slamming the door.

"Were you followed?" she demands to know.

"Followed? No, I don't think so."

"You don't think so? Jesus Christ! You were supposed to call, not come here and anyway, I thought you had to finish working on the damned picture."

"The situation changed."

"No doubt Linda will be glad to hear it. And by the way, where the hell is she?"

I watch as she walks over to a table on which sits a glass half filled with an amber colored liquid. She drains it and pulls open the top drawer. She takes a snub-nosed .38 from the pocket of her robe and places it in the drawer. I'm now picking up all sorts of vibes and I don't like the feel of any of them. My gut tells me I have just stepped into a snake pit.

"I don't know. I haven't seen her in several days."

"My old man says the packages arrived but she didn't."

She looks me up and down impatiently, expecting me to say something.

"I don't know what you're talking about," I tell her. "Linda sends me a note at the hotel. I wait until Thursday and call the phone number and reach the Red Sombrero. I figure that's where Linda is so I drive here. Now you say she's not here and you start talking about your boyfriend and a bunch of packages."

She picks up a pack of Luckies from a nearby table and lights up, then blows a billow of smoke in my direction.

"Not my boyfriend. My old man. My father Willie. I've got this little getaway place in Escondido. Pops lives there and takes care of it for me. Once a month I drive up and kick back for a couple of days."

"These packages, will they be safe there with your father?"

She grins.

"Pops owns a 12 gauge shot gun and a .45 revolver and he knows how to use them both."

"I'll take your word for it," I say.

"But, yeah, maybe I better get up there tonight and do something about the merchandise."

"What about your customers? Your regulars?"

"What do you mean, regulars?"

"You know what I mean," I say, trying to put her on the defensive.

"Well, you're wrong about that, buster. I hustle drinks for a fat fuck named Sal Santiago and that's all I do. Me and Linda that's what we both did before she up and ran off three years ago."

"And why did she do that, Rhonda?"

"Because Sal wanted to get in her knickers just the way he once tried to get in mine except what I did was bring a box cutter into the bed with me and I threatened to cut off his johnson then and there if he didn't leave me be. He almost crapped on the sheets and that was the last trouble I ever had with him. Linda wasn't like me. She was scared and instead of fighting back, she ran for it and ended up in Yuma."

"And you kept in touch."

"We kept in touch."

"So what about these packages?" I ask.

Rhonda regards me suspiciously.

"Just what is it you do know, Army?" she asks as she refills her glass from a bottle of cheap no-name whiskey.

"Nothing. She said she wanted to run away, that she had a way to make a lot of quick money. I said I couldn't get away immediately which she said was okay, that I could catch up later. The next thing I know, she's gone and I have a note in my key box. That's what I know and it isn't much."

"Then you don't know about Reese," she says.

"No. What Reese? What are you talking about?"

She just looks at me.

"Shit," she mutters, deeply concerned. "Where the hell is she?" She looks at me hard. "She didn't say anything to you?"

"No, I told you."

"Maybe they got to her before she could get out of town. Maybe she gave up Escondido. Pops could be in a lot of trouble. I definitely gotta drive up there tonight."

"I'll go with you," I say.

"No."

"I've got a gun, you've got a gun. If there's trouble, two is better than one. But I'd like some answers."

She thinks long and hard. Finally she says, "I can duck out around ten o'clock. It's about a forty minute drive."

"Okay," I say. "And the answers?"

"Army, trust me. The less you know the better off you are. Now I gotta go to the club. You wanna stay here?"

"I want to get something to eat. I'll meet you back here at ten and I'll drive."

"Whatever," she says.

Fifteen minutes later, we walk out of the building together. She goes east to the Sombrero, I head toward a joint I spotted a couple of blocks in the other direction. Wang's Wok is on the low end of the gastronomical chart. The orange chicken is rubbery and the fried rice is barely edible but I'm hungry. Even so I am able to leave half the calories on my plate. Bunny would be proud. I had planned to kill a couple of hours here but the smells are more than I can abide so I pay the check and take a walk over to the Navy Pier which juts out into San Diego Bay. There's not a lot going on but the sun is starting to settle onto the western horizon and I find a bench where I can relax and gather my thoughts.

These thoughts are troubling at best. Linda had seized on some sort of get-rich-quick plan and had shipped packages secretly to an obscure address in Escondido. In her duties for the cantina she had driven back and forth across the Mexican border in a panel truck bringing across tomatoes, eggplants, avocados, cases of beer and God knows what else. It is a minor crossing and she is a regular. No doubt she knew the border guards by name. She was passed through without inspection. Do I have to be a genius to guess what she'd been up to? Fast forward to a week ago. For reasons unknown she is tortured and then shot in the back of the head. Her murder screams Mob! and Mob! screams drugs and drugs scream Mickey Cohen, the criminal kingpin of Los Angeles. Sure, he may currently be in Alcatraz but I'm told by some of my substance using acquaintances that Cohen's organization is as active as ever. On the other hand, Rhonda didn't mention Cohen, she talked about a guy named Reese, whoever the hell he is. It seems inconceivable that Linda could have been involved with drugs but seven years is a long time and people change, especially if they're desperate. I have no clue as to how this all comes together but on the way to Escondido, I will make damned sure that Rhonda explains it to me in detail. I'll also tell her the truth about Linda and why she hasn't shown up to claim her packages.

It's quarter to ten and darkness has settled in. Street lights illuminate the area as I get up from the bench and head back toward Market Street and Rhonda's apartment house. In the distance I hear the wail of a police siren and as I turn the corner I see a squad car, it's roof light array blinking, parked in front of her building. A second squad car pulls up and two cops jump out, pushing their way through the gawkers who have already started to gather. I tap the shoulder of a guy on the fringe of the crowd.

"What's going on?" I ask.

"Not sure," he says. "Three shots. I heard 'em myself. I was across the street buying smokes. I walk over and this old lady comes out screaming. The super, I think. She's yelling murder and then somebody else comes out and I think he said there were two of them. A guy and some woman on the second floor. That's all I know, buddy."

I nod and start to elbow my way closer to the front of the building. Just then an ambulance arrives and backs up to the steps and a couple of guys in white coats jump out and race into the building carrying a stretcher. I try to edge closer but the cops are keeping everyone away. A minute later the ambulance guys reappear with a woman on the stretcher. It's Rhonda. She doesn't look good but she's still alive. They get her into the ambulance and it takes off, lights flashing and siren wailing. I get close enough to one of the cops to ask where they are taking her. He tells me Mercy Hospital. I tell him I heard there was another victim. The cop shrugs. The other guy is waiting for the meat wagon.

# CHAPTER SEVEN

**B**y the time I get to Mercy Hospital Rhonda has already been taken into the operating room. Still using Army McLeod's name I pass myself off as her brother. I'm told by the head nurse to take a seat in the O.R. waiting room and the doctor will come out to talk to me as soon as he can. I take a seat but I don't sit for long. I begin to pace,. Whether it's nerves or outright fear I don't really know but Linda Vasquez is dead and Rhonda Scanlan might soon be and there's a male stiff who came to Rhonda's door carrying armament, something he will no longer be doing. Whether he came as an emissary from Mickey Cohen or someone called Reese or maybe even Miguel Moreno I do not know but I do know I am in danger of being caught in a crossfire of competing bullets and I don't like it. Not one bit. I punish myself by buying coffee from a vending machine and pay the price. It tastes like a palpable substitute for rat poison. With a sigh I resume sitting in a straight backed chair and inadvertently close my eyes.

The next thing I know I am being gently shaken by a bald guy in green scrubs decorated with brownish blood.

"Mr. McLeod?"

I open my eyes and then struggle to my feet.

"I'm Dr. Kelvin," he says, "and the surgery went well. Your

sister's been moved to a room on the third floor and she's resting comfortably."

"Good to hear," I say.

"She's a lucky young lady," he says. "The bullet pierced her abdomen but missed all the vital organs. I expect a quick and complete recovery."

"Excellent. Any idea when I can talk to her?"

"Well, as I said, she's sleeping now and she was heavily sedated. I don't expect her to awaken for at least six hours."

"It's really important that I talk to her."

"Sorry. Can't be helped. I told the police the same thing. If I were you I'd go home and get some sleep and come back around seven."

"No chance before that?"

"None," he says. "I'll see you in the morning".

And with that he walks off.

Now what? I check my watch. It's half-past midnight. I could drive to Escondido and try to find Rhonda's little hideaway in the dark. Most all-night diners have phones and where there's a phone there's a directory. Provided it's not unlisted, I should find a telephone number and a street address for an R. Scanlan or a W. Scanlan. On the other hand I don't want to go knocking on Pops' door at three in the morning and get a load of buckshot in my butt for my trouble. There's a chance the old man's been compromised but between the shotgun and the .45 he should be safe enough until morning. I'll take the chance.

I turn on the Bernardi charm and learn from the supervising nurse that Rhonda has been assigned room 337 and there is a comfortable waiting room at the end of the corridor. I am reminded that the patient has been sedated and cannot be disturbed. I say I understand completely and head out. A few minutes later I settle into an easy chair in the new waiting room where a TV set with volume muted is showing Val Lewton's 'The Body Snatcher' with

Boris Karloff. You don't have to hear the crappy dialogue to follow the story and for a few minutes I am mesmerized. Then I start nodding off, waking up, then nodding off again. Each time I awaken Karloff is among the missing and some guy in a checkered sport coat is trying to sell me kitchenware.

I finally doze off for good around one-thirty and I stay asleep until I awake with a start around five o'clock. The movie has changed to a skinny Frank Sinatra in 'Higher and Higher' but the guy in the sport coat remains. I get to my feet, go to the doorway, and stare down the corridor. The floor is deathly quiet. I spot a couple of nurses but they aren't paying any attention to me. I start casually down the hall until I reach room 337 where I push on the door and step inside.

The room is dimly lit and Rhonda is lying in her hospital bed, an IV drip in her arm. Maybe an antibiotic, maybe morphine or some other pain killer. The monitors above the bed display her vital signs and everything looks stable. I pull up a chair bedside and watch her closely. Her breathing is normal, her visage peaceful. I ignore an impulse to wake her but I want to be right here the instant she comes to.

A few minutes to six she starts making mewling noises as she stirs. Her eyes open slowly, looking around to get her bearings. Her head turns and she sees me.

"Army?" Her voice is weak and labored.

"Good morning."

"Where am I?"

"Mercy Hospital and you're going to be fine. The doctor guarantees it."

She frowns.

"Hogg?" she says.

"What?"

"Kurt Hogg. He was standing in the doorway—" She breaks

off trying to remember.

"He's in the morgue with a tag on his big toe, Rhonda. You shot him."

She nods.

"As soon as I saw him, I knew what I had to do. I pulled my gun from my jacket pocket just as he was reaching for his. I hit him twice, I think, and then I think I caught one in the belly and I felt myself falling and that was it."

"Who was he, Rhonda?"

"Miguel Moreno's muscle on loan from the Cohen organization. I looked into his face and knew something had gone wrong. What's happened, Army?"

I take her hand in mine.

"First of all, I'm not Army. My name is Joe. Joe Bernardi." Fear flashes in her eyes. I squeeze her hand. "Don't be afraid. Army McLeod and I have been friends for years. I'm only here because he told me that Linda was missing and he was in trouble. Right now Army's in Yuma in the custody of the county sheriff."

"Custody? Why? What for?"

I still have a firm grip on her hand.

"Rhonda, I'm sorry. Linda's gone."

"Gone?"

"Dead. Someone killed her." She's shaking her head in disbelief. "They may try to pin it on Army but they can't make it stick."

"How? How did it happen?"

"She was shot. A bullet to the back of her head."

"Oh, God, I knew she couldn't handle it. I told her so. She was too soft to go up against those people. That poor dumb kid, all she wanted was out."

Tears start to form in Rhonda's eyes. The tough babe is beginning to melt.

"You're not supposed to be in here, sir!"

A sharp voice has emanated from the open doorway. I turn. It's a redheaded nurse with a scowling face. As she marches toward us I see her name tag reads 'O'Hara'. She also said 'sore' for 'sir' so I get to my feet, screw up my most abjectly apologetic expression, and feed her a bit of a brogue which I have picked up after years of being affectionately browbeaten by Bridget O'Shaugnessy, our housekeeper.

"I am so sorry, sister, but I was just after tellin' my dear sister about Ma and her ailments and how the doctor has given us the news and bad news it is, I'm afraid. We are talkin' days, sister, when Ma will be in the arms of sweet Jesus and the Blessed Mother and I had to come and tell dear Rhonda how it was goin' to be."

Nurse O'Hara grasps my hand and looks into my eyes.

"Ah, forgive me, sir. Just doin' my job. You stay now and I'll see that you're not disturbed and I am so very deeply sorry for your trouble."

And with that, she scoots from the room.

I look back to Rhonda.

"Now that we have the room to ourselves, why don't you tell me about Linda and her grand plan."

"Yeah. Why not? What are they gonna do? Kill me? Miguel Moreno's been supplying drugs to Mickey Cohen's organization for years. He made Linda a part of it right from the start. It was a perfect set up. The border right next door, the cantina and the catering operation in need of produce. She'd make a weekly trip to San Luisina for beer and whatever was in season and bring back marijuana or heroin or cocaine hidden in the cabbages, whatever Cohen's people were looking for. No one ever bothered her, everybody liked her. Cohen would send a truck to pick up the stuff in Yuma or in the case of a movie company on location, he'd have someone on the crew as a go-between."

"You're saying someone on the Phoenix crew works for Cohen?"

"I don't know that for sure but it's usually the way Cohen works on location shoots. He's had his tentacles in the movie business for a long time."

"So where did Linda fit into all this?"

"She was approached- don't ask me how- by a guy named Tootie Reese, a honcho in a gang known as the Crips. Reese runs the drug trade in East L.A. and his operation is big. He'd like it better if it was bigger and Cohen's was smaller. He persuaded Linda she could make a big score by dealing with him and not Cohen. It didn't take much persuading. Like I said, she'd had enough of Miguel who liked to use her for punching practice. She just wanted out so she agreed. Last week Miguel gave her cash to make a buy for Cohen. Instead she bought cocaine and marijuana for Reese, packaged it in cartons marked blankets and towels and had it shipped by UPS to Escondido. That's when and where she was supposed to disappear but obviously she didn't make it." She falls silent. "Coming after me, they must have done terrible things to her to make her give me up."

"They did," I say quietly.

"And Pops. They'll be going after him," she says.

"Maybe."

"Not maybe, Joe. You gotta protect him. You gotta warn him."

"My next stop, Rhonda. Where do I find him?"

She tells me, giving me precise directions and I promise to do whatever it takes to keep her father safe. I give her hand a final squeeze and duck out just as a nurse is coming coming down the corridor approaching Rhonda's room with a huge syringe on a metal tray. She gives me a suspicious look which I ignore as I hurry to the elevators.

The trip north is uneventful and I exit I-15 just south of Escondido onto West Valley Parkway and then to Harmony Grove. Rhonda's little hideaway sits on two acres in a sparsely populated area on the outskirts of the city. I keep a sharp eye out for a mail-box marked 'Scanlan' and finally find it after a couple of wrong turns. Next to the mailbox is a yellow and black sign which reads: NO TRESPASSING. Beneath is the warning: 'Armed Army Vet with Mean Disposition on the Premises.' I drive down the dusty dirt driveway to the front of the house and park. It is one story, old and constructed of clapboard and the whitewash exterior has turned to a splotchy grey over the years. A screened in porch spans the entire front of the dwelling. Just beyond to the right is a chicken coop and nearby the coop is a hog pen with three porkers wallow-ing about in their own swill.

As I get out of my car, the wind starts to whip up and sand and dust and debris are flying everywhere. Just then the screen door to the porch opens and a white haired old man in dungarees and a stained tee shirt steps out onto the stoop. He's carrying a double barreled shotgun.

"Turn around and git, mister," he says to me. "You got no busi-ness here."

"I just left your daughter a couple of hours ago, Mr. Scanlan. She sent me." I shield my eyes which are beginning to tear up from the dust.

"You one of her fancy men, sonny?"

"No, sir. I just met her tonight. She's in the hospital, sir. She was shot last night at her apartment."

"Pig sty."

"Sir?"

"She lives in a pig sty. No fit place for a decent girl. Saw the place once. Don't ever want to see it again." He waves the gun. "Keep your hands where I can see them."

"She's going to be all right. Thought you'd want to know."

"Assumed she would be. If she was dead or dying you'd have said as much."

72

"I've come for the packages, Mr. Scanlan."

"You mean the blankets?"

"That's right. The blankets. Maybe if you could lower that gun, sir. It's making me nervous."

"It's supposed to," he replies keeping the barrel leveled at my gut. "Last night it got real cold in the house and I thought about opening one of those cartons and taking out a blanket and then I thought again and decided that probably wasn't a good idea. What do you think, son?"

"I think you're right."

"Thought as much. You sell drugs for a living, sonny? Those cartons belong to you?"

"No, sir, they belonged to a young woman who wasn't as lucky as your daughter and no, I don't sell drugs. I want to get them out of here because as long as they are on the premises, Mr. Scanlan, your life is in danger."

"I can take care of myself."

"Ordinarily I'd agree but these are not ordinary people."

"Well, you're welcome to take them cartons. Don't want 'em around. They're stacked up just inside the front door. Me, I'll be fine."

I nod and start for the house. I'll resume the argument when I have the packages safely in my car. There are three cartons, good sized, maybe fifty pounds each, and they are hard to handle by myself. I drop one of them and slip and fall to the ground trying to lift another into my trunk. Sweaty and exhausted it takes me about fifteen minutes to secure them in the trunk of the Ford. Twice I get light-headed and once I actually fall onto the dusty dirty driveway. I think maybe my heart's acting up, but no, I'm finally able to slam the trunk lid without further incident. I turn back to Willie Scanlan.

"Mr. Scanlan, I strongly suggest you come with me. It's possible some very ugly people will come here looking for those cartons and when they ask you where they've gone to, they won't be polite about it."

"If they come, son, they won't get much closer to the house than you did and if they want to make an issue of it, they'll be dead or I will. Now get going."

I can see it's useless to argue so I open the front door of the car, then look over at the old man. I have one more card to play.

"She's in room 337 at Mercy Hospital in San Diego. You might want to stop by," I say.

"I might," he says.

"Rhonda pumped two fatal slugs into the guy who shot her but he may have friends who will feel obligated to finish the job. Hospital security can only do so much but a man in the waiting room with a revolver in an ankle holster watching her room, well, not many people would get past that kind of arrangement."

"Be even better if this person camped out in her room." Willie Scanlan suggests.

"Have to be a close relative for that to happen," I say.

"I expect so," Willie replies.

I nod and slip behind the wheel, then drive off. As I look in the rear view mirror I see him still standing, watching me go, shotgun in hand. If he stays and Cohen's minions show up in force he hasn't much of a chance but I admire his guts. I rather suspect that within the next few minutes he'll be in his car on the road to San Diego. Meanwhile I come to a crossroad with a sign reading 'Escondido 1 mile' and an arrow pointing left. I turn left.

The town's bigger than I expected. In fact it's actually a city. A sign at the city limits pegs the population at 115,600. Who knew? Anyway I have no time to sightsee and I keep my eyes peeled as I drive slowly down a main thoroughfare in the business section. And then I spot it up ahead on the left. The sign reads 'Keefer's Moving and Storage. Facilities Available By the Month'.

I pull into their parking lot and go into the office. The guy behind the counter is short and skinny with red hair and freckles and his name tag reads 'Rusty'. I tell him I need a unit and he is happy to oblige.

"Size?"

"Small," I say.

"If your items are really small, I can keep them under lock and key in the back room. Only seven-fifty a month."

"No, I want a unit."

"D is the smallest. Six feet high, four feet wide and twelve feet deep with shelving on the back wall. The rate's twenty a month in advance."

"Sounds perfect," I say, handing him a Jackson.

He shoves a rental agreement at me and asks to see my ID. I reach into my wallet and take out another twenty. I hold it up and tell him, this is my ID. He plucks it from my hand, retrieving the rental agreement.

"You been in a fight or something? You're pretty messed up," Rusty says.

"Or something," I reply. "Could we get on with this?"

"What was that name again? Johnson?" he asks, the pen in his hand hovering over the paper.

"Right. Johnson," I say. "Henry Johnson."

He nods and writes.

"You sound like you're from San Francisco," he says.

"You have a good ear," I tell him.

Scribble, scribble, scribble. Then he rubber stamps the form and hands me a small plastic keypad. "Unit 21," he says. "On your left toward the back. You can drive right up to it."

"What the hell is this?"

"Your remote. Your code is 4646. Enter it, push the button, the door lifts up and the interior light goes on. When you're finished, step outside, the door closes, the light goes out and the door closes and locks."

"Whatever happened to good old fashioned keys?" I ask.

"Worse than useless," Rusty says."People kept forgetting to return them so we had to keep changing the locks. Sometimes two or three units a day. Now all we do is change the code. No hassle and a lot cheaper."

"I'll take your word for it," I say, slipping the remote into my trouser pocket. "4646?"

"4646."

"Thanks," I say.

"See you in a month," he says.

I drive back to Unit 21, manipulate the remote and the door slides up and out of the way. I stash the goods on the rear shelf, step out and close the door. I give it a tug just to make sure. It's secure,.

A few minutes later I'm on the road, heading back to Yuma. The packages are safely stored and somebody, most likely in law enforcement, will be picking them up within a month. Henry Johnson believes in doing his civic duty. Henry Johnson is also now safe from harm or so he believes.

# CHAPTER EIGHT

I pull into Yuma a few minutes past four and make straight for the Coronado. I'm tired, sweaty, dirty and dusty and in bad need of a shower. I walk into the lobby and head straight for the desk where I ask the clerk if Mr. McLeod has returned to the hotel. He tells me he hasn't but officers from the Sheriff's Department showed up shortly before eight o'clock this morning with a warrant to search his room. I don't like the sound of this. I ask how long they were here. Not long, the clerk tells me. Whatever they were looking for, they must have found it right away. Despite the way I must smell, I turn on my heel and head back to my car. The shower will have to wait.

Sheriff Dixon is not glad to see me and even less so when I ask to see Army whom he is still holding.

"Not possible, Mr. Bernardi. He's conferring with his lawyer and after that, well, we're pretty strict about visiting hours."

"Which are?"

"Eleven thirty to noon," he replies with a smile. "Come back tomorrow and I'll try to fit you in."

"Has he been charged with anything?"

"Not yet. I'm waiting to hear from the county prosecutor."

"And the search of his hotel room earlier today? What was that all about?"

"Procedure."

"Meaning?"

"Meaning you are a civilian, Mr. Bernardi, and this is a police matter."

"In other words, none of my business."

"In my opinion," he nods.

"Well, Sheriff, I may be in possession of certain critical information that might bear on your investigation but at this point I don't feel it incumbent upon me to share it with you. In my opinion."

He gives me a steely look.

"You could be skating on thin ice here, Bernardi," he says.

"Yeah, I guess I could be," I say. "I'll just wait outside for Ms. Garcia."

I exit the building and find a spot on a bench by the sidewalk. Fifteen minutes later Angelique emerges and I get up to intercept her.

"Angelique, what's going on?"

"Nothing good, Joe. I think the county attorney is getting ready to charge him. Murder one."

"That's insane."

"Come on, I'll buy you a drink." she says and we start down the block. She gives my disheveled wardrobe the once over. "What happened? You get in a fight or something?"

"Or something," I say

At the corner is an unprepossessing bar called Shelley's. Inside it is dim and quiet. Two guys are chatting at the bar. Another is sitting at a table nursing a beer and reading the morning paper. His jacket is unbuttoned and I can see the grip of a holstered revolver under his armpit. Angelique and I slip into a booth.

"This is cither a mob hangout or a cop bar," I say dipping into the trail mix.

"The latter," she says. "Also a smattering of lawyers and courthouse clerks. After five o'clock it gets a little raucous."

The bartender comes around from behind the bar.

"Hiya, Angie. What'll it be?"

"Rye neat, Shelley. Water back."

He looks at me.

"Coors?" I ask.

"Corona," he suggests.

I nod and he walks away.

"So what's the bad news?" I ask.

"They found a.22 pistol under the mattress in Army's room. Ballistics has already made a match. It's the gun that killed Linda."

"Of course it is," I say irritably. "And of course, no prints. It was wiped clean."

She smiles.

"You should be a cop."

"Sometimes I think I am. The guy's not in his room for several days, anybody with a passkey can get in and what moron wipes away his prints and then hides the weapon under his mattress where even Elmer Fudd could find it?"

"My thoughts exactly," she says.

"And the Sheriff?"

"He knows it stinks but Army's all he has until he can dig up somebody better."

"And who's the judge in this town? Roy Bean?" Bean was a hanging judge in the 1800's, self-promoted as 'the law west of the Pecos.'

"It's not that bad," she says.

"You sure about that? I have information that may bear directly on Army's case and I'm afraid to pass it on to Dixon. God knows whose pad he might be on."

We shut up for a moment as Shelley returns with our drinks. As soon as he walks away, Angelique says, "Tell me what you've got."

"Not sure I should. You're an officer of the court. You might feel obliged to share it or worse, be forced to."

"I can take care of myself."

"I'm sure you can."

"This information you have, would it involve persons who habitually exhibit unlawful behavior regarding proscribed narcotics?"

"It would and that's as far as I'm going to go for the moment."

If she's annoyed or offended she tries not to show it. That's the lawyer in her. Never let 'em see you sweat. Never let 'em see your cards. She fails miserably. At the mention of drugs her face fell almost imperceptibly and her eyes lost their luster and became dead.

She reaches in her purse for a pack of Chesterfields and taps one out. I take the matchbook from the ashtray and light it for her. She doesn't bother to thank me.

"I'm sorry I can't be more forthcoming," I say.

"You do know we're on the same side," she says, inhaling deeply.

"I assume so."

"Good, because at the moment you're making me feel very unnecessary."

"I don't mean to," I say. "There is something I can mention. What do you know about a man named Kurt Hogg?"

"Miguel Moreno's trained gorilla? What's he got to do with this?"

"That's what I'm trying to find out."

"Nobody knows much about him," she says. "He's from L.A. and he works at the cantina as a kind of host when he's there which isn't often. Six months ago he was picked up on a charge of seducing a 12 year old boy. A lawyer arrived the next morning from Los Angeles and the charges were dropped by nightfall. I have a feeling this wasn't the first time Hogg was caught diddling a prepubescent kid. You might want to ask Sheriff Dixon about that."

"Be delighted to but the Sheriff doesn't feel we have much to talk about."

"So Hogg's involved," she says with a knowing smile, "which means that Moreno is involved."

I grin and waggle a disapproving finger at her. I decide she doesn't need to know that Hogg is dead, at least not yet.

"Can't shoot me for trying," she says, sipping her scotch.

We spend the next twenty minutes chatting aimlessly. She knows all about me. My life is chronicled in less than 200 words on the dust jackets of both my published books. I learn that she is a graduate of Arizona State, studied law at UCLA, was married at 21 and divorced at 24. No kids but lives with a younger sister, also divorced, who works as a hairdresser at a local salon.

"So, will you be sticking around?" she asks.

I nod.

"Until this situation with Army is resolved."

"In that case, can I interest you in a home cooked meal this evening?" she asks and her eyes signal that she is talking about a lot more than meat loaf. In my younger days I would have arrived early bearing all the requisite groceries. Today at 45 I wouldn't risk Bunny for the crown jewels of England. Still I don't have to be a boor about it. I reach for her hand.

"Angelique—"

"Skip that. Now it's Angie," she says.

"Angie, that is the most gracious and tempting invitation I have had in years. Regretfully I must decline. For one thing I have to go out to the movie set and pitch in, if needed. Army would do the same for me if our positions were reversed."

"And tomorrow evening?" she suggests slyly.

"Well, here's the problem. We did one of those family ancestry things on my wife Bunny and it seems she is a direct descendant of a woman hung in Salem, Massachusetts, in the 1600s and she has a gift - perhaps you'd call it a curse - which makes her privy to everything I think and everything I do so for the sake of domestic harmony, I do nothing and I think nothing and we get along just fine."

She stares at me for a moment and then breaks out in laughter.

"That is the most priceless bag of crap I have ever heard," she says.

"Yes," I say, "but it delivers me from temptation."

"Suppose I promise not to seduce you."

"Well, that's different. I'll bring dessert."

"Anything chocolate," she says.

"Done. And I'm partial to lamb chops," I say.

"Me, too," she says.

Let the games begin.

I arrive at the set a few minutes past five, park the car and then look around on the ground for a twig. Night shooting is on the call sheet. A midnight wrap is predicted. I don't really think there's much that Aldrich will need me for. Actually I'm hoping to catch the dinner break and rattle the newly minted widower's cage. That is, if Miguel is there. I suspect he will be. I wonder if he's learned by now of Kurt Hogg's demise. I hope not. I want to see his face when I tell him.

The supper tables have been put out, the aroma of garlic and broiled beef and fried fish fill the air. Out by the plane the scene has been wrapped. Sherry Banks, the production assistant, is helping out the script supervisor by taking polaroid shots of all the actors before they head for supper. This is to ensure that nothing has changed when they resume filming after the break. For example if Dan Duryea were wearing a bandana around his neck and removed it for some reason while eating and then forgot to put it back on, most of the film shot after supper would be useless. Medium two shot, wearing bandana. Close up, no bandana. Slip ups like this have been known to drive producers to drink. Polaroids solve the problem.

I find Aldrich and describe Army's predicament as best I can, letting him know that for a couple of days I'll be available to pitch in if needed. I ask him to keep our conversation confidential. Army's situation is tough enough without wild rumors flying about in every direction. Aldrich says he understands completely.

I return to the catering truck, grab a tray of ravioli and find a spot between Ernie Borgnine and Ian Bannen. Both inquire about Army. I say I have nothing concrete to tell them and they don't press me. Conversation turns to the brand new baseball season. Ernie and I disagree about the merits of the Dodgers versus the Cardinals. Bannen, a Brit, tries to follow the conversation but is hopelessly lost and wanders off in search of hot tea.

"I've been meaning to ask you," Ernie says. "About the girl in New York. The one you were protecting while we were shooting 'Marty'. Whatever happened to her?"

"Bunny? I married her."

Ernie's face breaks into a broad toothy grin.

"Terrific, Joe. Just terrific."

"And as long as she behaves herself I'm going to keep her," I dead pan.

Now Ernie laughs out loud. I look past him to the truck where Miguel is handing out beverages while Luigi and Maria work the grills and the stovetop. For a grieving widower, Miguel seems to have made a quick and painless recovery from his loss and when the a.d. Cliff Coleman finally hustles everybody back to the set, I hang behind. By now Miguel is scraping off trays and hosing them down. I walk over to him, handing him my tray.

"Very sorry about Carlotta, Miguel. She seemed to be a lovely person."

"Thank you, Mr. Bernardi. You are most kind, but I wasn't aware that you'd met her, " he says between scrapes.

"I was told."

"I see. You were told." He fixes me with a curious look.

"Are you planning any sort of service?"

"The funeral home just got her body from the authorities. I am thinking maybe tomorrow they will arrange a viewing for her many friends. After that, cremation. She was not a religious person and neither am I."

I nod.

"I understand. It must be hard to be so shorthanded. Is Kurt handling the cantina?"

He looks up at me sharply.

"You know Kurt?"

"I've heard his name mentioned and uh, wait. Now I remember. Someone said he was out of town. Not good timing, considering the circumstances."

"Company business. He had no choice."

"San Diego?"

"What?"

"I think they said he was needed in San Diego."

"And exactly who told you that?"

"No idea. Somebody on the crew, I think. Have you heard from him?"

"What?"

"Has Kurt checked in with you? If it was an important business matter, you must have heard from him by now."

He's squirming and I'm loving it. He knows I know something but he's not sure where I fit in so he's keeping it low key.

"You're very curious about my affairs, Mr. Bernardi."

"Not at all. You've just suffered through one traumatic event. It would be devastating to face another."

"Meaning what?"

"Meaning nothing. It's just been my experience that fate plays cruel tricks just when we least expect them. And if you haven't heard from him who knows whether your friend got to conclude his business? Perhaps he was hit by a car in a freak accident. I admit I'm overly cautious but that's just me. A born pessimist. I'm sure he's just fine. Great meal this evening, by the way." I smile as I turn and start walking toward the plane. I can feel his eyes boring into my back and the Beretta in my trouser pocket feels very comforting.

For the next thirty minutes I hover next to Corey, the sound mixer, a friendly guy from Nebraska who's been at this for fifteen years. Is this Cohen's mole, inserted into the crew to facilitate the drug buys? Or maybe it's Digger Jones, his muscle-bound boom mike man from New Zealand. If there is a Cohen mole embedded in the crew, and that's a big if, chances are he or she is a junkie. Hard drugs are no respecter of age, sex, color or gender and junkies, otherwise decent people, will do anything to perpetuate their habit.

My eyes float across the various crew members wondering which one, if any, is working with Miguel Moreno. Since no one is wearing horns or sporting a forked tail or cloven hooves, I give it up pretty quickly. Then out of the corner of my eye I see the catering truck leaving the premises, heading back to the cantina. I check my watch. Eight-forty-five. Time for me to split as well.

When I get back to my car I go around to the trunk to check on the small twig I jammed between the trunk lid and the chassis. Not there. I find it lying on the ground. I bend over and look closely at the lid lock. If I weren't now expecting to find them, I might have missed them but they are there. Faint, almost microscopic, scratches on the chrome caused by a jimmying tool. I pop the lid. Nothing has been disturbed except maybe the mood of the intruder who looked for, but did not find, a cache of drugs.

I pull into the Coronado parking lot at nine-fifteen ready for my much needed shower and a good night's sleep. Tomorrow is Sunday. A day off for the movie company. I wont be needed. I walk over to the desk to pick up my key and see a message in my box. The clerk hands it to me, saying a man left it just a few minutes ago. I unfold it. It reads: 'Join me for breakfast at the cantina tomorrow morning at nine. We have much to discuss. MM.'

I slip the note into my jacket pocket and head for my room. I am so good at cage rattling, sometimes I even astound myself.

# CHAPTER NINE

Long ago I learned to walk and chew gum simultaneously which is why I am leafing through a copy of 'Yuma Today: Where to Go and What to See" all the while dialing Mercy Hospital in San Diego. When I'm connected I ask for Room 337. It's early the following morning. I risk waking her but I need to know she's okay.

"Yeah?"

A gruff man's voice. It's either Pops or an ill-mannered doctor.

"Willie?"

"Who's this?"

"Joe Bernardi."

"Oh, yeah. The drug dealer."

"I am not a drug dealer. How is she?"

"Asleep."

"Don't wake her."

"Never crossed my mind."

"Last night I poked around in a rattlesnake pit, Willie," I say. "Could be someone unfriendly might come looking for her."

"They'll find me."

"They'll be armed, Willie."

"That'll make two of us."

"You smuggled weapons into her hospital room?" I ask in

disbelief.

"Just the shotgun and the .45. I'll be fine. My girl will be fine. Anybody else I can't answer for."

I almost laugh but I don't. Willie would take it the wrong way but now I am pretty sure that Rhonda is in good hands.

"Tell her I called."

"I'll do 'er," Willie says and I hang up. Immediately, I dial another number and after three rings, Miguel Moreno picks up.

"Moreno."

"Bernardi."

"Ah, amigo. It's ten past nine. I've been waiting for you to come through the door."

"I'm sure you have but you see, Miguel, I checked your ad in the yellow pages and you don't open on Sundays until eleven o'clock for lunch."

"I have planned a private breakfast."

"And that's the problem, a little too much private togetherness for me."

"You have no need for concern."

"You know that is so good to hear but I'm going to grab some waffles in the hotel dining room."

"But sooner or later, Mr. Bernardi, we will have to meet." His tone is now measured and ominous, oozing intimidation.

"Great," I say cheerily, referring to my open copy of the Yuma guide to activities. "Suppose we meet at the Territorial Prison Museum at two clock."

"I don't think I want to—," he starts to say.

"I do," I say firmly. "You want to meet, here's your chance. Or we can forget it."

"I'll be there," he says.

Just before two I drive to the end of Prison Hill Road and park near the entrance. The parking area is about half full which is fine by me. The more tourists about the better. The prison dates from the late 1800's when Arizona was a territory and it has always had a reputation as a bleak and brutal place. No doubt the heat had a lot to do with it but there's no question, looking at its foreboding walls, it was not a place you'd check into voluntarily. Today it's a tourist attraction with a visitor center, gift shop and museum. Two years ago the feds closed down Alcatraz and I'm wondering how long it will take them to turn the Rock into Disneyland in the Bay. If they do, Yuma will be next.

Moreno is waiting for me just inside the visitor center from which the guided tours emanate. I figure we'll skip the history lesson and get right to it. We grab coffees from the snack bar and sit down at a table.

I smile at him, raising my paper cup full of coffee in a silent toast.

"So did you ever hear from Kurt?" I ask.

"A mutual friend told me he ran into some trouble in San Diego," Moreno says.

"Sorry to hear it," I say. "Nothing serious, I hope."

"Terminal."

"Too bad. I never had the pleasure of meeting him. So, on to other things. You know, Miguel, if you needed to look into the trunk of my car, you merely had to ask me for the keys. I'm a very obliging fella."

"I'm glad to hear that," he says, "because I believe you have something of mine."

"Do I?" I ask blankly.

"Yes and I'm willing to pay handsomely to get it back."

I shrug. "I wish I could help you."

"Oh, you will," he smiles. "Sooner or later."

I smile back.

"What I really wanted to talk about was your wife, Carlotta, who was not exactly your wife but why split hairs? God knows how it happened but my good friend Armitage McLeod is being held by the county sheriff on suspicion of murder and I believe it's only a matter of hours, a day at the most, before he will be formally charged. Of course, it's perfectly ridiculous and you and I both know it, don't we, Miguel?"

"I know nothing about who is responsible for Carlotta's death. If I did I would kill him with my bare hands," he says, giving a good imitation of indignant anger.

"That's too bad. I was counting on you, Miguel, I really was. Not that I wanted you to confess, no, that would have been too much to ask for, but I'd hoped you might supply a name, maybe just a hint in the right direction."

"Careless talk, Mr. Bernardi. Careless and dangerous."

"Well, the trouble is, someone has spent great effort to frame my friend for her death and it has affected my judgement. I do and say things I shouldn't, make rash accusations. A terrible failing on my part but when it happens I can deal with nothing else."

Moreno fixes me with a look that borders on contempt. "I have associates who would consider you a very dangerous person to let run around loose."

I perk up.

"Associates. Excellent," I say smiling broadly. "I love associates. When can we get together?"

"I realize, Mr. Bernardi, that you are toying with me and if this is the way you wish to proceed, I cannot stop you. I can only warn you. Return my goods and that will be the end of it. You may leave Yuma in peace and return to your wife Bunny and your daughter Yvette. I suggest you take advantage of this option."

I fight hard to keep from tossing my coffee in his face. Instead I get to my feet and stare at him coldly.

"Obviously, you weren't listening. I want the son of a bitch that murdered Linda Vasquez and I don't care who he is or how I

90

get him but I will get him and Army McLeod will be released and then maybe, just maybe, my faulty memory may clear up and I'll remember what happened to your so-called goods. However if anything should happen to my family, I can guarantee you will never see your goods again and even more to the point, you personally will never see the first of next month."

I give him one last hard look, then turn and stride toward the entrance and out of the building and into the clear but stifling Arizona air. I don't take the time to breathe it in. I hop in my car and race back to the hotel. I have a phone call to make and it won't wait. It rings twice and a woman picks up.

"Faubus Security," she says.

An answering service. Of course. It's Sunday.

"Listen carefully," I say. "This is literally a matter of life and death. Tell Mr. Faubus that Joseph Bernardi has to speak with him immediately. Make sure you say immediately." I give her the number at the hotel and my room number and tell her I expect a callback within the next twenty minutes. I hang up and stare at the phone as if it were a lethal weapon. I pray to God that Zeb's not out on his boat or at the ball game or stretched out on his chaise on the back patio dead asleep. I get lucky. None of the above. Twelve minutes later the phone rings and I pick up.

"This had better be good. Edna's off visiting her sister and I've got a hooker in the guest room."

I laugh out loud. Next to Army, Zeb Faubus is the most straight-laced guy I know. He gets flustered by underwear ads in the morning newspaper.

"Tell Miss Mattressback you're busy with a desperate but very wealthy client."

"Sounds like trouble to me," he says.

"The worst kind."

"Yeah, I never did like Arizona. What's in Yuma?"

"Long story but I need round the clock security at the house."

"Not a problem. We've done it before," he says

And indeed we have. Twice when Jill Marx, the mother of my daughter, was still alive. Twice my activities had put her and Yvette at risk and twice Zeb had thwarted the danger.

"Who have you pissed off this time?" he asks.

I tell him what's going on. When I mention Mickey Cohen and drugs and the gang leader Reese from east L.A. I can sense the tension on the other end of the line.

"You're fucking with serious people, Joe," Zeb says.

"I know and it's possible they won't come at me through family but I can't take the chance."

"No, you can't. Have you talked to Bunny?"

"Not yet. She's next."

"You gonna tell her the truth?"

"Hell, no. As far as she's concerned there's been a rash of burglaries nearby and people have gotten hurt. We're just being cautious. It's temporary."

"As good a lie as any. I'll have two men at your place by five o'clock. They'll recheck the systems and spell each other until tomorrow morning. Then we'll start a three man rotation. You still got that bodyguard-chauffeur?"

"No, we let him go a few months ago. Really didn't need him."

"Then I'll give you a fourth guy on weekdays to drive the kid back and forth from school.

"Good."

"Call Bunny,. Tell her to expect us."

"Will do."

I hang up and immediately call home. Bunny answers, glad to hear from me, and we exchange pleasantries and dirty sex talk. Finally I get around to the point of my call and I glibly repeat the nonsensical story about break-ins and bodily harm. Bunny's radar is impeccable and I realize immediately that my words are not getting through. I keep at it because to tell her the truth about drugs and Mickey Cohen and a vicious gang member would send her into a rage, not of anger, but of fear. At the moment, truth is not an option so I stick to my story in the hopes of wearing her down. I half succeed. She agrees to keep an open mind. Not so my daughter Yvette who is aghast at the thought of being driven back and forth to school instead of being permitted to interact with her gal pals on the school bus. The situation is 'grotty' (grotesque) and I am an ogre. She gets off the phone in a snit. Bunny gets back on, snitless but still wary. When I tell her Zeb's boys won't be around more than two or three days she feels better. For all her carping, I realize that the security situation isn't really what's bothering her. She misses her honeypie (me) and she won't be happy until I'm home again. This is what I tell myself. Whether it's actually the case, I have no idea.

Angie has called leaving a time, an address and a phone number and at six-fifteen I pull up in front of a high-end apartment building on W. Water Street close by the Colorado River. I walk into the lobby carrying a small white box containing a half dozen chocolate eclairs. The guy at the security desk is expecting me and after I sign in, he directs me to the elevators. Fourth floor. Number 4D. He'll call up and let her know I am on my way.

I push the buzzer and a half-second later the door opens and I realize immediately that I am in Angelique Garcia's crosshairs. I was promised that sex would not be on the menu but here she is, her raven hair falling loose and provocatively onto her shoulders and her body swathed in white silk lounging pajamas. The smile she tosses me completes the picture.

"Welcome," she says.

"Thanks," I say, handing her dessert. I step inside and look around. The living room is decent sized, decorated in earth colors and warm and inviting. "Very nice," I continue. "Your outfit as well, Angie. You must be a very neat cook. Not a stain or a grease splatter in sight."

"That's because I don't cook. I invited you for a home cooked meal, Joe. I didn't say I was going to cook it. Come in the kitchen and meet my sister Josie."

We go in the kitchen and I meet a junior sized version of Angie wearing a sweater and jeans and mashing up several boiled potatoes in an oversized pot. We are introduced and I say everything smells terrific which it does and then I notice that the table in the alcove is set for two and I wonder why Josie isn't joining us. Turns out she and her electrician-boyfriend Kenny are going to catch the seven o'clock showing of 'Doctor Zhivago' at the local nabe. Now more than ever I regret having left my chastity belt back in my hotel room. Tonight promises to be a good exercise in character building which reminds me of Bunny which reminds me I need to call home to be sure that Zeb Faubus is on the job.

Angie points me to a phone in a small room which serves as a den, library and emergency guest bedroom. As soon as Bunny gets on the phone I am treated to an earful.

"What robberies? What break-ins?" she asks. "I checked with a couple of the neighbors. They think you've been drinking."

"Zeb told me—"

"Zeb is lying through his teeth," she says. "He says it's just routine but he's triple-checking all of the systems and plans to leave two men overnight, one outside, one in. If that's routine, I'm Lady Bird Johnson. Joe, what's going on?"

"Bunny, I told you—"

"Stop treating me like an idiot. Who do I call to get the truth? Aaron? Ray? Mick? Any one of the three? Am I the only one who doesn't know what's going on?"

"Okay, okay," I say. "I may be in a little bit of trouble with some unsavory characters." I go on to tell her what's happened, minimizing the danger aspect. When I finish she says she feels better that she knows but emphasizes that she is getting tired of my penchant for playing cops and robbers. I'm a middle aged man with a family and I should start acting like one. I promise to come home safe at the first opportunity I get to extricate myself from this mess. At heart I am not Dick Tracy, just a plain ordinary family man who would rather leave the troubles of the world up to someone else.

In my zeal to convince Bunny that I am safe and well, I have lost track of Angie who now comes up behind me.

"Joe, I forgot to ask, what do you want to drink?" she asks.

"Who's that?" Bunny asks sharply.

"Beer," I reply in response to Angie's question. "Army's lawyer," I say in response to Bunny's.

"Lawyer? Sounds more like Betty Coed. Where are you?"

"Her place."

"Her place." she repeats.

"We're about to have dinner?"

"Dinner. Right. Where's Army?"

"In jail."

"Just the two of you then."

"No, her sister's here."

"Thank God for that," Bunny says.

"Bunny, it's dinner, that's all. Just dinner."

"Did I imply otherwise?" Bunny replies, all innocence, which is when I realize she is yanking my chain.

"Are you having fun?"

"Loads," she says. "Joe, sweetheart baby, there are three things I can count on in this world. Death, taxes, and my husband's fidelity."

"Meaning you take me for granted," I say.

"I do, and before you start getting all unraveled, that's a compliment, handsome. Now you and Periwinkle Mason sit down to supper while I bust Zeb's chops for bullshitting me."

"Call me later," I say.

"You can count in it," Bunny says and hangs up. I smile. Come hell or high water, we're stuck with each other til death do us part which is just the way I want it.

Josie serves the lamb chops at six-forty, Kenny arrives at six-forty-five and Angie and I are deep into our meal and chatting like magpies by seven o'clock. She has a dry and wicked sense of humor as she tells me all about her adventures at Arizona State and her ex-husband who was a mistake in every way beginning with his aversion to work and his enthusiasm for tequila. After dinner we move into the living room with coffee and eclairs and I begin to subtly query her about the principal players in Yuma starting with Sheriff Joshua Dixon.

"If you mean, do I think he's honest, yes, I think he is. Do I think he's a bigoted son of a bitch? That, too. Indians. Hispanics. He doesn't show it to me because I'm well connected but if you're just some guy off the street and your name ends in a Z, you get looked at real hard."

"Does he know his job?"

"Barely. Bottom line, he's a book cop and he doesn't make many mistakes because he doesn't do much and while he's prejudiced, he tries to keep it out of his work. The truth is, he's better at getting elected than he is actually doing the job." She lights up one of her Chesterfields and looks at me curiously. "Something you want to share with me, Joe? Now would be a good time."

"Angie, what I know is incendiary. It could burn you," I say.

"I've been burned before."

"I need you to keep this to yourself, at least for the time being."

"I'll try my best but as you once said, I'm an officer of the court. Some things I may be obliged to reveal, if asked."

"I'll take the chance," I say. "If you're going to be hanging around me, you have a right to know."

I tell her all of it. Rhonda and the shooting of Kurt Hogg in San Diego, Willie Scanlan standing guard in her hospital room, me having stashed a large quantity of drugs in a safe place, my conversation with Miguel and his not-so-veiled threats against my family and finally the dangerous ganglord from East L.A. Tootie Reese who has yet to make an appearance but most certainly will.

"And that," I say to her, "is why I asked you about Sheriff Dixon and what I can expect from him if things should get out of hand."

"You mean like getting blown away in a dark alley some night?" Her tone is suddenly harsh and bitter. I've hit a nerve.

"That won't happen, not as long as I have the drugs in my possession."

"Well, good luck with that, Joe," Angie says quietly. "Don't you know most of these animals will give up a score just to make a point when their machismo is threatened."

"I don't think it works that way," I say.

"You don't, huh?" She laughs bitterly. "And just when we were getting to know one another."

# CHAPTER TEN

The Monday call at the location is eleven o'clock which means everyone will breakfast in town and lunch will be served on the set between three and four. More night shooting is in the offing and a midnight wrap is likely. I roll in along with everyone else shortly after ten o'clock, well rested after a good night's sleep. Angie delivered on a terrific dinner and I artfully avoided anything else, finding myself back at the hotel before ten o'clock, my virtue intact but totally out of gas from the events of the past couple of days.

I've had a busy morning. At quarter past eight I had called my good friend, Lt. Aaron Kleinschmidt of the LAPD at his home. Aaron is a major cog in the Homicide Bureau and I had high hopes of gleaning some much needed information.

"Hello."

His voice sounded tired. I was afraid I'd wakened him. Nonetheless I got right to the point.

"With Mickey Cohen doing a stretch on the Rock, who's in charge of his operation?"

"Bernardi? Is that you, Joe? Jesus, do you know what time it is? I haven't even had my coffee yet."

"That's why I'm not wasting time with small talk, Aaron, so you can get to your breakfast."

"Very considerate of you," he said, "and what kind of trouble is your sorry ass in now?"

"None you need worry about."

"Oh, you and Cohen's people are planning to sponsor a church social together, is that it?"

"It's a simple question, Aaron."

"And are you likely to get yourself killed?"

"Not likely but you never know. In any case I absolve you from the obligation to send flowers. Now, about the Cohens."

I heard a long sigh when he realized I wasn't going to go away.

"You and your fucking death wish," he mutters. "Jackie Bloom is the acting boss but he's more a bookkeeper than anything else. His wife Nedda is the muscle. She's been married to the mob since she was 19. Three marriages, the first two ending violently to make room for number three. She and Jackie have been married seven years, a match made in gangster heaven. He keeps the books, she keeps the peace and underlings cross her at their own peril. Now, what the hell are you up to?"

"I'm involved in a sort of situation." I'd told him.

"God damn it, Joe, you're always involved in a situation and this sounds like the worst one yet. Mickey Cohen. You do things in a big way."

"Thanks, Aaron. And while I have you on the phone you could also tell me what you know about Tootie Reese."

"Oh, my God," he'd sputtered and the conversation went downhill from there. He devolved from anger and admonishment to offering police protection which he couldn't do since I wasn't in L.A. Finally I thanked him profusely and hung up. Aaron thinks of himself as my big brother, very protective of my well-being, all a part of atonement for trying to frame me for murder many years ago when he was a small cog in a very corrupt police department. Now he's a good cop and a better friend but I am sure the guilt will never leave him.

I snap back to the present and get out of my car. The catering truck is just pulling in to its usual spot. Miguel is behind the wheel, Luigi next to him. I don't see Maria. She could either be in the back peeling tomatoes or back at the cantina, serving lunch. I suspect the latter when the truck rolls to a stop and an unfamiliar figure steps out of the rear door. He's heavyset but not fat and boasts thick black hair atop an olive complexion. By now Miguel is out of the cab and looking in my direction. He waves with a smile. I'm reminded of flies and spider webs.

I check inside the production tent, grab a copy of the call sheet, and touch base with Aldrich who is pretty sure I won't be needed today. I take a Nehi from the cooler and walk back outside which is when Miguel grabs me by the arm.

"Let's take a walk," he says.

"Over what cliff?" I respond.

"You're much too nervous, Bernardi. Relax." He leads me a couple of hundred yards away into the nearby desert scrub where we can't be overheard, then stops. "I think I have a solution to our problem."

"Good to hear."

"The gentleman with us today—Mr. Bloom—was a close personal friend of the late Mr. Hogg. He's been working at the cantina for the past couple of weeks."

"I hadn't realized," I say. "Bloom. Any relation to Jackie Bloom?" I ask.

"You know that name."

"I've heard it."

"Marcus is a cousin, I believe," Miguel says. "Anyway several days ago Mr. Hogg mentioned to Marcus Bloom that he, Kurt, had made several advances on my wife, all of which were rebuffed. The final one was the day of her death. Apparently Hogg was determined to conquer Carlotta in the back of the cantina and she was just as determined he wouldn't. She produced a gun, they struggled and the weapon discharged accidentally, killing Carlotta instantly. Hogg was terrified of facing me with the truth so he put her body in the trunk of his car and drove out to the desert where he dumped her body within a half mile of the movie set. He left undetected and returned to the cantina where he removed any trace of the altercation. End of story."

"And quite a story it is, Mr. Moreno."

"Marcus will swear to it, the sheriff will believe it and your friend will be released."

"Ah, were it that simple," I say. "You know, Miguel, I'd be half convinced to believe that load of crap if it weren't for the fact that Bloom has been nowhere near Yuma the past few weeks, the lady was covered with a dozen or more unexplained cigarette burns and Kurt Hogg was far more interested in diddling eight-year-old boys than getting into the undies of a 30-year old woman, no matter how attractive."

"I'm trying to help, Bernardi. I take it you still want your friend exonerated. This does it."

"I also want the guy who did the killing and you're wasting my time until you turn him over."

"You insist on doing this the hard way."

"Yeah, I guess I do."

Miguel shakes his head sadly.

"I am a businessman, Mr. Bernardi, nothing more. My associates, which include Marcus Bloom, are much more than that and operate within a code that you and I would find abhorrent. Nonetheless it exists and while I could dismiss my financial loss in this matter as a life lesson, these people I deal with not only have endured life lessons many times over, they often inflict them."

"In other words, play ball or end up on a sand dune."

He shrugs.

"I cannot protect you from them. Cooperate. Please. Enough blood has been shed."

I shake my head.

"I'll cooperate when you deliver the person who killed the woman you called your wife. Not until."

I turn and walk back toward the huge tent with a bravado I do not really feel. He calls after me.

"You were warned, Bernardi! You were warned!"

As I pass by the catering truck on the way to the production tent, I can feel Marcus Bloom's eyes on me. Outwardly I ignore him. Inwardly I am scared shitless. I slip my hand into my trouser pocket and wrap it around my .25 caliber automatic. It gives me little comfort.

I hang around for another half hour, ignored by everyone. Unneeded, I go to my car and drive back to the city. I have things to do and people to talk to.

First on my list is an obligatory call to Bunny at her office. We exchange hellos, she asks how I'm doing, I say okay but it's complicated, she asks when I'm coming home, I say maybe a couple of days and maybe longer, we say we miss each other and I know we do, and finally after a couple of 'I love yous' I hang up. I feel rotten. I don't like being in Yuma, I don't like what I'm embroiled in. I want to be safe with my family back in L.A. and enduring great frustration, I know I can't until I get things resolved. If only Army McLeod hadn't telephoned me.

My next call is to Rhonda Scanlan and she picks up right away. She's not chipper but she sounds better.

"How are you feeling?" I ask.

"Okay. The doctor says another couple of days and I can leave."

"Very good news."

"The cops were here yesterday."

"What did you tell them?"

"A load of crap. I told them the guy Kurt was an old boyfriend who'd once threatened to kill me. As soon as I opened the door he grinned and reached for his gun. I pulled mine and we fired simultaneously. Self defense. I think they bought it."

"No problem with your gun?"

"I have a carry permit. The club got it for me on account of all the undesirables I have to deal with."

"Is your Dad still there with you?"

"They booted him out yesterday. A nurse spotted the shotgun."

"So nobody's watching out for you."

"No."

"Damn it," I mutter.

"Not to worry, Joe. The nurse didn't see the .45. It's under the mattress where I can grab it right away."

"I don't like it, Rhonda. You're a target."

"I can handle myself, Joe."

"I hope so."

When I hang up I am still worried. Armed or not, she's at risk. I think it's time to pay a call on the sheriff. It's pushing four o'clock when I slip behind the wheel of my car and pull out into Fourth Avenue. A white Mustang parked curbside across the street pulls out into traffic, does a U-ey and parks itself on my tail. I don't think much of it until I take a left turn and he does likewise. An immediate right turn and he's still there. I've picked up company. I squint into my rear view to get a better look at the occupant. I'm pretty sure there are three of them, all blacks, and all wearing blue bandanas on their heads. I casually slow down and then, when they are close, I speed up enough to be able to read the car's front license tag. RDM381. I commit it to memory as I pull into the Sheriff Department's parking lot. The white Mustang keeps going, turning at the next corner. As I start inside I see that Angie's VW is parked by the door.

I go inside and instead of getting a stall or the runaround, I am escorted directly to Joshua Dixon's office. It's almost as if he expected me. He points to a chair, inviting me to sit, and then he leans back, eyeing me curiously.

"Maybe you can help me, Mr. Bernardi, because I'm getting very curious about something. Your friend, McLeod, has a very sharp lawyer. I've had him locked up for three days now although I haven't arrested him and yet, Miss Garcia has not presented me with a writ of habeas corpus. Why do you think that is?"

"Didn't we discuss keeping him here to make sure he's safe?" I say.

"Safe from what?" Dixon asks. "Something's going on here, Bernardi. Garcia knows. I don't. Fill me in."

"I came here to do just that, Sheriff, with the lady's permission."

"She's in with him now. She shouldn't be much longer."

"Good," I say. "In the meantime I have a couple of things you might want to check out. There's a man up at the movie location by the name of Marcus Bloom. He's working for Miguel Moreno. Bloom is tied into Mickey Cohen's organization. Might have a yellow sheet, might not. You could probably get a mug shot wired down here from the LAPD. Also I was followed here from the hotel by a white Mustang carrying three black men wearing blue bandanas. That's the insignia of the Crips gang in east Los Angeles."

"And what have they got to do with this?"

"Quite a bit. The plate number is RDM381."

He stares at me for a few moments, then picks up the phone and orders a subordinate to phone Los Angeles for anything they have on Marcus Bloom. He also asks to be connected with the Motor Vehicle Bureau, then hangs up and looks over at me.

"I get that you don't like me, Sheriff," I say.

"Not the issue, Bernardi. You're probably an all right guy, but you're a buttinski, you stick your nose where it doesn't belong. I do the policing around here. You should stick to writing your fairy tales."

"It's a matter of priorities, Sheriff. Protecting Army McLeod is at the top of my list. I'm not sure where he fits on yours."

"I do my job," he says just as the phone rings. It's the Department of Motor Vehicles. He gives them the plate number, says he needs a call back a.s.a.p. As he hangs up, there's a knock on his door. It opens. Angie looks in.

"We were just talking about you, Miss Garcia. Come in and sit down," Dixon says. She gives me a curious look, then shuts the door and takes a seat. "Mr. Bernardi has something he wants to chat about but he needs your okay."

Angie looks over at me.

"I talked to Rhonda," I say. "The San Diego police bought her story but the hospital ejected her father from the premises so she's alone in her hospital room and unguarded. I think we need to bring her here for protection and to do that, we need to fill the sheriff in."

She nods.

"I have no problem with that," she says.

And so I go through the story once again, bringing Joshua Dixon into our little circle, all the while praying that he is only a bigoted boor and not on Mickey Cohen's payroll. When I finish I lean back in my chair. So does Dixon.

"Drugs," he says in disgust.

"I didn't open any of the boxes but I assume so," I say.

"Where are they now?"

"Safely stashed away," I reply.

"Specifically?"

"I can't help you. Not yet. Right now I am the only person who knows where they are and the only person who can lay hands on them. For my own peace of mind, I want to keep it that way."

"They're evidence, Bernardi."

"And if and when all this comes to trial, I'll make them available. Until then, my secret."

He takes a long thoughtful pause.

"All right, for now we'll do it your way," Dixon says.

"What about Rhonda Scanlan?"

"What about her?" Dixon asks.

"She can exonerate Army McLeod, at least to the extent that he knew nothing about the drug deal."

"Hearsay."

"I'm not talking trial here, Sheriff. I'm talking investigating this murder. You know as well as I do that McLeod is a big harmless teddy bear. You've got a planted gun and no motive and maybe Rhonda can fill in some missing pieces and you can start chasing after the actual killer."

"Okay," Dixon sighs. "You get her here, I'll put her in protective custody and she can tell what she knows to the county prosecutor."

"You might have to make some calls to San Diego."

"I'll make 'em," Dixon says. "Hard to believe. Mike Moreno. Always thought he was one of the good greasers. Now its drugs and maybe murder. Shows you can never tell. I guess once a greaser, always a greaser."

I look over at Angie who has been very quiet. Her expression says it all.

The phone rings. Dixon picks up.

"Dixon." Pause. "Uh huh. Got it." He writes something down. "Thanks," he says and hangs up. He looks over at me. "White Mustang RDM381, registered to a Thomas Reese, Address in east L.A. You're getting to be a very popular guy, Bernardi. First greasers, now spooks. Who's next?"

Angie and I take our leave. I for one am glad that I am not a Jew, a raghead or a Chink because if I were I doubt I could get Dixon to talk to me. I assume he doesn't have anything against Wops or maybe he just doesn't realize I'm Italian. It's now ten past five, too late for a trek to San Diego and besides it's unlikely I can get Rhonda released from Mercy at that time of night.

"Supper?" Angie asks as we walk to our cars.

"We did that last night," I say.

"And look how well it worked out."

"That it did but I'm turning in early tonight so I can leave for San Diego at dawn."

"I'm going with you," Angie says.

"No, you are not," I tell her.

"You may need some legal muscle springing her from the hospital. I specialize in legal muscle."

"It could be dangerous," I say.

"I'll chance it."

"I said no."

"Fine," Angie says. "Tell your lifelong buddy to get himself another lawyer."

With that she peels off toward her Volkswagen.

"I'm leaving at six sharp," I call out as she reaches for her door handle.

"I'm an early riser," she says.

"I do the driving," I tell her.

"I couldn't care less."

"Be in the lobby at quarter to six or I'm leaving without you."

"I'll be in the coffee shop at five-thirty having breakfast," she says.

"That'll work also."

"All right."

"All right."

And with that she drives off. having been told exactly where she stands. Joe Bernardi, master of the art of persuasion. That's me.

# CHAPTER ELEVEN

The following morning I'm in the lobby at precisely five minutes past six. Angie is waiting impatiently by the entrance to the coffee shop holding a brown paper bag. She makes a show of checking her watch as I approach.

"You're late. Let's go," she says.

"I haven't had my breakfast yet."

"I have."

"My alarm clock malfunctioned."

"Mine didn't. We're behind schedule."

She starts for the front entrance. I tag after her.

"This is unfair."

"Life's unfair." She shoves the paper bag at me. "Here's your breakfast. Come on."

She exits and I follow, taking time to peer into the bag. One container of coffee. One jelly doughnut.

"You call this breakfast?"

"No, I call it an act of charity on my part. You want me to drive while you eat?"

"No," I growl as we reach the car. I slide in. I leave Angie to open her own damned door. A few minutes later we are heading west on Rte. 80. I am driving with the paper bag on my lap, the coffee container in my left hand while I drive with my right, all the while trying to figure out how I am going to get at my jelly doughnut without cracking up the car.

We cross over the Colorado River and bypass the Fort Yuma Indian Reservation as the road subtly starts to rise. We're approaching California's Cuyumaca Mountains and the landscape is nothing to look at. The traffic is moderate. I try the radio to little avail. After twenty minutes we lose the Yuma stations and after that we get nothing but static. Except for some aimless chit-chat, mostly we've been silent. I learn that Myrna's absence from her desk the other day was family related. She had to fly to Phoenix to post bail for her mother, a 42 year old street-walker who apparently remains a fine looking specimen of womanhood. It's a profession she drifted into many years go when secretarial school proved to be both boring and unpromising. Apparently she had promised Myrna multiple times that she would quit the business but never did. She claimed it was because she met so many interesting people. I don't know quite what to say about that so we lapse into silence for several more minutes.

"Look, Joe," Angie says finally, "if you want to stop for a decent breakfast, it's okay by me."

"I'll keep my eyes peeled for a Howard Johnsons," I say, not very gallantly.

"I guess I deserved that. Sorry."

"Forget it," I say.

"Didn't get much sleep last night," she says.

"Nervous?"

"Pissed off."

"At me?"

"No, not you, Joe. They killed him, Joe. My husband Jeremy."

"Who killed him, Angie?"

"Not who. What. He graduated from tequila to drugs. Heroin.

Cocaine. Jerry wasn't fussy. Anything to help him forget he was the worthless fourth son of a tyrannical oil company executive. Glad Hand Harry Somersby, everybody's friend, everybody's buddy and the evilest son of a bitch I ever met. When Jerry died last year in Oakland, Harry told the authorities to cremate him. He couldn't even be bothered to bring him home to Tulsa." She chuckles. "Too bad I met Harry after Jerry and I were married. I knew he was a prick the minute I laid eyes on him."

"Sorry," I say.

"What for? He's God's handiwork, not yours. The drugs may have killed Jerry but they had a lot of help from Glad Hand Harry. Don't know which I despise more."

"Guess you don't have much use for Linda Vasquez then," I say.

"Actually I feel sorry for her. I can only imagine how desperate she had become to get involved with those people, scared stiff, not knowing how to get away. She paid a terrible price, Joe, and I'd like to even the books for her and put those evil bastards in prison for good."

"For Jeremy."

"And for me."

"You realize you're probably talking Miguel Moreno."

"Never one of my favorite people," she says, turning her head to view the monotonous scenery. The silence resumes.

Ahead the sky is darkening and I suspect rain lies in wait. It is only quarter past seven. A roadside sign reads 'S1 North 1 mile'. A minute later, as I approach the intersection, I see a Gulf service station and check the fuel gauge.

"We need gas," I say.

"Good," Angie replies. "I need a potty break."

I pull my rented Ford Fairlane up to the nearest pump and a fresh-faced kid probably a few months out of high school bounds out of the office. I tell him to fill her up with high test and check

110

the oil. He's eager to pitch in and I head for the office in search of more coffee and at the very least, a bag of peanuts. As breakfast the jelly doughnut didn't cut it.

The grandmotherly clerk at the register is pleasant and obliging. The coffee is hot and only forty cents a container. At the candy rack I grab my peanuts as well as a Three Musketeers and a Mars bar for later.

"Where ya headed?" the old lady asks.

"San Diego," I say.

"Be a while," she says. "Big accident up ahead just past the Pine Valley cut-off. They're sending a helicopter up from Mercy Hospital in San Diego. Radio says a couple of people are bad hurt."

I grimace. The last thing I need is to be stuck in traffic for hours.

"Anyway around it?" I ask.

"Yep. Kinda out of your way."

"Tell me."

"Get off at Pine Valley Road, head north all the way to Rte 79, then turn south and you can pick up the 80 again on the other side of the accident."

"No chance of getting lost?"

"Not unless you're deaf, dumb and blind."

The kid walks in and announces he's pumped twelve dollars and ten cents worth of gas. I hand Grandma fifteen bucks and hand my change to the kid. Just then I look out the window and spot the white Mustang which has just pulled into the station. The driver gets out leaving two companions still in the car. He's a big black man, solid, and sports a blue bandana. No doubt in my mind, this is Tootie Reese. He is looking at my car thoughtfully just as Angie emerges from the ladies room and heads for the car. I turn to Grandma.

"Don't panic," I say, "but the men in the Mustang are drug dealers and they have followed me here. They won't bother you but they sure as hell want to bother me."

"I've got a .45 peacemaker under the counter," she says enthusiastically.

"No. No shooting." I turn to the kid. "What's your name?"

"Wendell," he says.

I hand him a five dollar bill.

"Okay, Wendell, here's what I want you to do. Go the car casually, wipe down the windshield, then get in and drive it over here right next to this doorway. Then get out and come inside which is when I am going to jump in the car and pull out before they have a chance to figure out what's happening. Can do?"

"Can do, sir," Wendell says as he ducks out. I turn to Grandma.

"These guys are going to come after us. Don't think they'll bother you but whatever you do, don't mention the Pine Valley exit."

"No worry there, son," she says.

"And then after they've left you might want to call the local police or the sheriff or whoever's in charge and get 'em to pick these boys up."

"No worry there, either. White Mustang RDM381," she says. "Got those fellas nailed."

I look outside. Wendell is swinging the car around toward the door with Angie in the passenger seat. I get ready to go, just inside the doorway.

"You take care now," Grandma says with a wink.

"You, too," I say as Wendell comes through the doorway and I go out. He left the driver side door wide open and the motor running so I jump in, slam the door and tromp on the accelerator aiming straight for Tootie Reese. Startled he stumbles backward and I miss him by a good foot. His jacket flies open revealing a pearl handled pistol stuffed in his belt. Probably not the smartest move I've ever made but I just couldn't resist. I peel off into the traffic on 80 as I hear a shot ring out. A bullet smashes the passenger side rear view mirror.

"What the hell was that!!!" Angie shrieks.

"You didn't recognize our friends from East L.A.?"

"Oh, Christ," she says looking back. "Looks like they're coming."

"I'm sure they are," I reply gunning it and passing a slow moving Plymouth, narrowly avoiding an oncoming pickup truck.

"And try not to get us killed."

"That's the general idea." I tell her about the accident ahead and the detour over to Rte. 79. "We'll lose about thirty minutes but we avoid the hassle."

"You're the boss," she says as I speed up to 80 to pass three cars before I see an oncoming vehicle and slide back into my own lane. I keep checking my rearview. I know they're back there, I just don't know how far.

Raindrops start to splatter on the windshield and the sky has turned much darker. Like it or not we are headed into a major rainstorm. Traffic is slowing now. I'm barely crawling and twice I've actually stopped. I keep looking back. Reese and his cohorts are nowhere in sight but it's small comfort. If traffic stops dead, bumper to bumper, Reese is likely to send one of his people forward to locate us. If the man has a gun, things could turn ugly.

The rain falls more heavily as we inch forward. I keep looking back. The road sign ahead which seemed so inviting minutes ago now seems miles away. To hell with it, I say to myself as I yank the wheel to the right onto the shoulder. It's narrow, barely wide enough for the Ford and on the other side is a precipitous ten foot fall off into the neighboring forest.

"When I said you're the boss, I wasn't including suicide," Angie says, cringing down in her seat and avoiding the view.

"Just hang on," I say speeding past stalled cars praying that someone ahead doesn't get the same brilliant idea and lurch out in front of me. But no, these are docile law abiders and I reach the turnoff without incident. It takes a couple of minutes to actually reach Pine Valley which is a quiet little mountain hamlet of 1420 people. The welcoming sign says so. I slow to 25 going through town because the last thing I need is to be pulled over for speeding. A sign at the far end of the town reads Guatay 3 miles and Rt. 79 8 miles. As we head into the rain swept wilderness we pick up speed. I'm pretty sure we've lost Reese and his cronies for good but even if they figure it out and double back I plan on being long gone.

The road is paved but it's no superhighway. The ruts and pot holes are many and well disguised. Reason and battered kidneys tell me to slow down. Panic prevents me. As the road climbs higher, it becomes more twisty and warning signs of impending curves are not always in evidence. Darkness closes in and suddenly sheet lightning flares up in front of the windshield and a crash of thunder reverberates all around us. I'm momentarily blinded and only at the last second do I realize I've come upon a sharp left hand curve. I turn the wheel and then feel the car skidding out of control on the wet surface liberally coated with mud and debris. I hear Angie gasp audibly as we spin around and then I can feel the car slide backwards, off the road and then pitching rearward down a muddy embankment. Jouncing and skidding the car defies control and suddenly rams to a stop as its rear crashes into an old and sturdy oak tree. I'm slammed back, then forward into the steering wheel. My head hits the windshield and recoils. I hear Angie cry out and then the car is still. Very still. She has been thrown into the dashboard and her head is bleeding. I feel warm wetness on my forehead and cheeks. I check. I, too, am bleeding.

"Are you all right?" I ask.

"Sort of," she replies, dabbing at her forehead and discovering blood on her fingertips. "Oh, great," she mutters.

The engine has quit so I turn the ignition key. I get a frantic click-click- click. I am no mechanic but click-click-click is not good news.

"Well, we can either hoof it," I say, "or stay in the car and risk being found dormant next week by some inquisitive bird watcher."

"And me in high heels," she says ruefully. She grabs the door handle and opens the door a crack. Wind and rain force themselves on her. Quickly, she slams the door. "We might consider waiting for a while in case the rain stops."

"When do you suppose that'll be?" I ask.

"Sometime this week?"

I nod. We sit quietly for several minutes contemplating our situation. And then the rain abates. Not completely but what remains is a soft drizzle.

"I'm game if you are," I say.

"What the hell. We can't stay here."

She opens the door and steps out of the car.

"Shit!" she shrieks.

"What is it?"

"Mud. Ankle deep!"

I open my door and look down. Mud. I peer at the back tire, covered up to mid hubcap. This car isn't going anywhere any time soon. I step out and sink into the glop up to my ankles. Even though the rain is light I feel myself getting soaked. I stare up at the road above us. I estimate ten to twelve feet and while there is some hillside vegetation, mud predominates. This is going to be very tricky. I'm not sure Angie can handle it.

I grab a protruding bush and pull myself up but I get little purchase with my feet. My wet hand slips and I slide backwards. Now I'm covered with slimy mud, my feet are wet and sloshy in my shoes and worst of all I feel myself laboring for breath. Memories of my visit to Jim McCaffrey come flooding back to me. Light exercise to start. No undue exertion. I suddenly have a picture of me lying face down in this mud, my ticker inoperative and some ambulance guy clicking his tongue sadly as he zips me into a body bag.

"Joe! Over here!"

It's Angie calling. I look. She's about thirty yards away and I can see that she is standing in a place where the roadbed is even with the top of her head. I get to my knees, then my feet and struggle uncertainly to get to her. I keep sliding and falling and then getting up and after a couple of minutes I reach her. Now my breathing is severely labored as I gasp for air.

"Are you all right?" she says, clearly concerned.

"I will be," I say. "I haven't had this much fun since basic training at Fort Sill."

"Can you make it?" she asks.

"Of course I can make it," I scoff.

"Then follow me."

She scrambles up the short embankment, using bushes and protruding roots for handgrips. I notice that her feet are bare.

"Where are your shoes?"

"God knows," she replies and then she's up and over, safe on the shoulder of the road. "Come on!" she calls to me.

Heavy-legged and breathing hard I try to pull myself up. I grab at a root. It is cold and slimy and wriggles out of my hand before it slithers into the underbrush. I'm pretty sure it wasn't a rattler. I look for a handhold and can't find one and now I am starting to feel a tightness in my chest as my breathing becomes more labored.

"Joe! Grab hold!" she calls out as a tree branch appears in front of my face. I grasp it tightly and pull myself up. Angie has a tight grip on the other end. As I near the road bed, she reaches for me and I grab her wrist as she grabs mine. With strength I had no idea she possessed, she helps me up and over the crest of the embankment. I roll over on my back, panting, drizzle washing my face.

"Let me guess," I wheeze. "You work out."

"Every day," she says. Then, "Are you going to be all right?"

"I just need to rest for a minute," I say, raising my arm to check my wrist watch. The face is covered with mud. I wipe it on my shirt and it's barely clean enough to read. 10:44. Mid-morning but overhead the sky is still dark. To the west I see bluer skies. A lot of good that's going to do now.

Angie is standing, looking both ways up and down the road. Clearly she's hoping a passing car will pick us up but considering how we look, I find that a distinct improbability.

"Car coming," she says looking westward toward Route 79. I look, too. I don't know what it was that warned me. Possibly the slowness with which the car was moving or maybe some primal instinct for survival.

"Down! Get down!" I scream at her reaching out and grabbing her slimy dress and pulling her to the ground.

"What are you doing?" she says struggling to get up. I grab her arm and keep her pinned to the ground behind some low lying shrubs.

"Lie still!"

The car approaches and then glides slowly by. It's a white Mustang. Tootie Reese is behind the wheel. One of his men is riding shotgun, the other's in the back. Maybe I'm nuts but I could swear the shotgun guy looked right at us but covered with mud, we blended right into the terrain, invisible in plain sight. The car continues slowly down the road headed toward Pine Valley. It shouldn't be long before they return, driving even more slowly.

# CHAPTER TWELVE

"Let's go," I say, struggling to my feet.

"Go? Go where?"

"Anywhere. We can't stay here. We have to find some kind of shelter."

I cross the road to the other side. Angie hurries after me. Her feet are bare and it's obvious that walking is no fun. On this side of the road, the land abutting the road is level and fenced with white boards. It looks to be grazing land but there are no animals in sight. We start walking in the direction of Guatay which I guess to be less than a mile away. I keep looking behind me for any sign of the Mustang. So far so good.

The road bends to the right and and as we come around the turn, I see the sign about fifty yards ahead. It's posted next to a driveway and reads 'Colin Cochrane Stables, Guatay, California. Lessons. Stabling by the Month.' It starts to rain harder. Angie and I pick up the pace and a couple of minutes later we are at the gravel driveway. At the end of it, about two hundred yards in, is a two story frame house and nearby, a barn and stables. There is no sign of a vehicle and my first reaction is, there's no one home. Nonetheless, Angie and I hobble down the driveway. Even if the house is deserted we can certainly find shelter in the barn or the stables.

I don't know how it happened. Maybe I tripped over something or a knee gave out or dizziness overwhelmed me but suddenly I find myself sprawled on the driveway. I hear Angie call my name and then she's kneeling down beside me, looking into my face.

"Joe, what is it? What happened?"

"Don't know," I say. "Must have slipped." My words but it doesn't sound like my voice. What the hell is going on?

"Are you hurt? You look terrible."

I grunt something unintelligible.

"Can you stand? We have to get to the house."

I try to move my legs. Nothing happens. I strain to make it happen. Nothing. Angie's face is pained and puzzled. I shake my head.

"I'm going for help," she says as she gets to her feet and starts to run toward the house. I try to call after her but my voice has been rendered silent. I feel dizzy. A pool of black ink swirls in my brain as my eyes close. All is dark. All is silent.

"Is he awake?"

"I don't know."

Two strange voices, a man and a woman. Time has passed. I don't know how long.

"Joe, can you hear me? Wake up."

Angie's voice.

Someone is patting my face. I manage to open my eyes. It's a man. Longish blonde hair and a short cropped beard, grey-blue eyes, leathery tanned skin, an outdoorsman.

"His eyes opened," the man says.

"Praise be to the Lord," a woman says. I cannot see her. Then she leans in over the man's shoulder. Plump, grey-haired, a heart shaped face.

"Daniel!" the man says.

"Yes, Pa." A new voice.

"Give me a hand. We have to get him into the house."

"Yes, Pa."

Strong hands tug at me and pull me to my feet, then I feel myself being half-dragged, half-carried toward the house. Out of the corner of my eye I can see Daniel. Young. Very young. Maybe fourteen or fifteen. Longish hair like his father, skinny, a bad case of acne. My head lolls and the ink in my brain returns.

"Lay him on the bed," the man says.

"He's filthy," I hear Angie say. "He'll ruin your sheets."

"Sheets wash out," the older woman says.

I'm laid on my back and the bed feels very good. I'd like to open my eyes but I can't.

"Let's get those clothes off him."

"I'll do it," the man says. "Daniel, take Jasper and ride over to Doc Leary's. Tell him we've got a mighty sick man over here."

"Yes, sir."

"You be careful now." The old lady.

Hands are unbuttoning my shirt. Others are tugging at my trousers. I finally manage to open my eyes. Angie is standing over me, wrestling with my shirt. She's wearing a wool bathrobe and her face has been scrubbed clean. I smile at her. Or at least I think I did. I can't tell any more.

"Lie still," she says. I do as I'm told. I have no choice. I close my eyes again, feeling nauseous. Now when I move I feel a stabbing pain in my chest. I'm aware of a warm cloth on my face, washing the mud away. It moves to my neck and shoulders. My pants are gone. So is my underwear. I know I'm stark naked and I don't care. Modesty is not an option. The cloth moves down my body to my private parts and then a blanket is laid upon me. All I want to do is sleep and I wonder, is this what I've finally come to? My last moments, away from Bunny and Yvette, tended to *in extremis* by strangers. I don't want to contemplate it. I close my eyes and try to shut out the world.

I'm aware that time has passed and I hear muffled voices. My blanket has been pulled aside and I feel something cold on my chest. I peek. A man with a wrinkled face and untamed pepper-and-salt hair is leaning over me, a stethoscope in his ears, listening intently.

"Doc?"

"Shhh."

He taps my chest with his fingers, then takes something from his medical bag and flashes it into my eyes. Finally he backs off.

"This man needs more attention than I can give him. Colin, can you drive him to Mercy in San Diego?"

"Can't, Doc. Car quit on me yesterday. Needs a new starter."

"I'd take him," the doctor says, "but I have to stick around. Maria Montoya's gonna deliver any minute now. What about Pedro? He available?"

"Don't see why not. Not many tourists about today. He won't be cheap," the man called Colin says.

"Our local taxi service," the doctor says, apparently to Angie.

"Money's not a problem," I hear her say.

"Somebody call him. We have to get this man to the hospital as soon as possible." As he says it he raises up a large syringe, checks to see it is clear of air bubbles and then jabs it unceremoniously into my gluteus maximus.

From then on everything is mostly a blur as I keep slipping in and out of consciousness. I am aware that I have been dressed in clean clothes. The socks and underwear are fine but the sweat pants are too short and the sweat shirt, also too small, bears the logo of the despised San Diego Chargers, I being a devoted fan of the Los Angeles Rams. Then I am being stuffed into the back seat of an elderly taxicab, Angie crammed in beside me. The driver seems like a jovial fellow, partial to the Hispanic music coming from his radio. He sings along and beats out the rhythm all the way into downtown San Diego. I feel as if I know the lyrics to Cielito Lindo by heart in Spanish, a language I do not speak.

Finally the cab stops. The rear door is thrown open. Two men dressed in white are tugging at me and finally get me settled onto a gurney. I feel myself being wheeled rapidly in through the entrance to the emergency ward. From then on it's more blur. Once again my clothes come off and I am wrapped in something akin to a tablecloth. Nurses and doctors fuss over me, taking my vital signs, talking over me as if I didn't exist. A dark skinned doctor seems to be in charge. He talks funny. I think of 'Gunga Din'. And then, after what seems like hours of this manhandling, I am wheeled into elevators and down corridors and finally deposited on a bed in a dim smallish room. I sense that I have been admitted for further treatment which is, of course, totally unacceptable. I have things to do and people to see. More black ink. The ink doesn't care what I want, it comes and goes whenever it pleases.

Sometime later, an hour or maybe just six minutes, a nurse shakes me from my slumber to administer a sleeping pill. I tell her I'm not interested. She tells me it was ordered by Doctor Shastri. I don't care.I tell her my doctor's name is McCaffrey and I want to see him immediately. She turns and hurries from the room. I'm afraid I have offended her.

Now I notice Angie. She is sitting in an chair in the corner, wearing a frumpy floral patterned house dress. She's watching me with a bemused look in her face.

"You really are a lousy patient," she says.

"Thanks," I say. "Cute outfit."

"Belonged to Colin's ex-wife. Left it behind when she walked out on him six years ago."

"Too bad. Who's Colin?"

"You really are out of it," she says.

"So how sick am I?" I ask.

"Sick enough," she says.

"And what the hell's that supposed to mean?"

She gets up and comes to the bed. She sits on the edge and takes my hand.

"The good news is, you didn't have a heart attack."

"Thank God for that," I say. "What was it, indigestion?"

"Anxiety. A panic attack. Your EKG was nothing to cheer about and the doctor says you're going to need plenty of rest. Your blood pressure is sky high and they've given you something to bring it down. "

"So I'll live."

"Only if you take care of yourself."

"Have you talked to Rhonda Scanlan?"

She shakes her head.

"Not here. Checked out yesterday."

"How? Why?"

"What do I look like, her long lost sister? They wouldn't tell me. Checked out, gone, end of story."

"No, not end of story. In the hospital, she was reasonably safe. How did she leave? With her father Willie? Where did she go?"

"I told you—-"

"East wing. Third floor. She was in Room 337. Find a nurse named O'Hara. She'll answer your questions. Tell her you're my sister-in-law from Guadalajara. I'm Irish. Our mother was dying. That's what I told her when she caught me in the room with Rhonda. She'll remember."

Angie gets up.

"Okay, I'll try," she says heading for the door.

"Angie, where are my clothes?"

"Mama Maybelle bundled them up for you and I've already taken them to an all-night laundry. They'll be ready by eight o'clock tomorrow morning, not that you're going anywhere."

"And, uh, what about my personal effects?"

She walks back to the bed, reaches in her purse and pulls out my wallet.

"Good," I say.

Then she extracts my trusty .25 caliber Beretta automatic.

"Better," I say.

"What exactly is it you do with this cap pistol?"

"Careful," I say, "you'll hurt it's feelings."

I put out my hand but she puts it back in her purse along with my wallet.

"I'll hold onto these for you," she says as she turns and hurries from the room. I am being treated like a six month old baby and I don't much like it.

I lay in bed, seething and impatient. No heart attack. Good. I'm getting out of here first chance I get. Good. Rhonda handled Kurt Hogg but she probably doesn't know that Tootie Reese is on the prowl looking for the drugs that Linda had bought for him and that's bad. He may know about Rhonda's involvement, he may not, but she has a right to know what's happening.

At least thirty minutes have passed when the door opens and a short little man in a white coat peers in. He sees me awake and throws me a toothy grin as he comes to my bedside.

"Ah, my friend, you are looking better. Amazing what a little sleep can do, am I not right?"

Yep. I had him pegged, all five foot four of him, slicked back greasy black hair, dark olive complexion and a name tag that reads I.M. Shastri. Gunga Din's illegitimate son, an expatriate from Bombay.

"You are feeling better, no?" he asks.

"I am feeling better, yes, Doc. When can I leave?"

"Leave? Oh, no, no, no. You need rest, my friend, and I must conduct more tests."

"But I have to get out of here."

124

"No, you cannot move. It is not possible."

"And if the hospital were burning down? I'd just lay here and broil like a fat chicken?"

"No, no. You are able to walk. You are not an invalid but I must keep you under observation. It is protocol."

"Screw your protocol," I say.

Just then Angie comes through the open doorway. Shastri turns to her.

"Miss Garcia, I implore you to talk some sense into your friend. He may not leave. He must stay and there's an end to it."

Thus saying, he leaves.

"Is pissing off everybody one of your major talents, Joe?" she asks.

"Top of the list, Angie. Top of the list. Now what did you find out?"

"Rhonda Scanlan left yesterday right after lunch, AMA, in the care of her father and it definitely was her father. Everyone on the floor remembered the shotgun."

"AMA? What's that?"

"Against Medical Advice. They can't hold you against your will, Joe. It's called kidnapping."

"So they've gone to Escondido."

"Apparently so."

"Tomorrow morning," I say. "I need my clothes here by eight o'clock."

"No."

"What?"

"I said, no. You're not going anywhere, Joe. You are not a healthy man. In your condition any activity could be very dangerous. I'm not going to watch you die."

"Irrelevant," I say. "Get me my clothes and you're out of it. Grab a bus back to Yuma. I'll handle Rhonda."

"Joe—"

"I'm doing this with or without you, Angie. I have to get Rhonda to Yuma, to tell Dixon what she knows about Linda's scheme. Otherwise Army is going to rot in some Arizona penitentiary and that is definitely something I do not owe him for once saving my life."

She stares at me hard. Maybe she thinks I'm kidding. I'm not.

"Okay. Eight o'clock," she says, "but I'm going with you to Escondido."

"Not a chance."

"Yes, I am," she says. "The Escondido police are going to need someone to identify your body after you've keeled over, Joe. In California, it's the law."

With that she stalks out of the room, trying to slam the door as she goes. She fails miserably. Heavy hospital doors do not slam, not in California. It's the law.

# CHAPTER THIRTEEN

Seven-thirty the next morning. I've been awake for over an hour. So far, no sign of Angie. A kitchen staffer has just brought me breakfast and I scarf it down as quickly as I can. Given the uncertainty of this morning's agenda, I'd prefer to function on a full stomach. Angie appears at ten of eight wearing her own newly cleaned outfit. She's got my clothes on hangers covered with brown paper. I smile at her. She neglects to smile back. I disconnect myself from my medical monitors and take my apparel into the bathroom where I quickly trade in my drafty backless gown for undergarments, trousers, and my favorite cashmere sport jacket. I am just slipping on my shoes when someone pounds on my door, jiggling the handle. Nurse Mackey, proficient in the use of long needles and devoid of any sense of humanity, must have been summoned by my beeping heart monitor which had informed her that I was apparently dead. I step back into the room and she looks at me aghast.

"Mr. Bernardi, what are you doing?" she gurgles, unable to believe her eyes.

"Leaving, Nurse Mackey, with gratitude for all you did for me yesterday."

"You can't leave, you're a patient!" she says frantically.

"I was. You cured me," I say.

Just then another nurse hurries into the room followed by an orderly and a few steps behind, Dr. I.M. Shastri.

"Mr. Bernardi! No, no, this is unacceptable," Shastri says anxiously. "You must return to your bed."

"No can do, Doc. I have places to go and people to see."

"You fail to understand, sir. You are a very sick man. Please do not force me to restrain you physically."

"Now, Doc, you can't do that and you know it."

Angie's purse is laying on the bed table. I pick it up and rummage around in it for my wallet and my pistol, the latter evoking gasps from the nurses before I slip it into my pants pocket. From my wallet I take out one of my Bowles & Bernardi business cards which I hand to Shastri.

"Send the bill for my treatment to this firm and it will be paid promptly."

"You are risking your life, sir," Shastri says.

"Mine to risk, Doctor. Thanks for everything. Come on, Angie, let's blow this fire trap."

She and I stride purposefully from the room with Shastri hurrying after us babbling about an AMA release form. I stop momentarily at the nurse's station and ask for a blank form, and sign it. I hand it to the doctor telling him to fill in the details.

When we walk out of the hospital into a clear sunshiny day, my watch reads 8:27. A cab pulls up and discharges its passengers. Angie and I hop in and tell the driver to take us to the nearest Hertz outlet. Escondido is a very long walk.

Thirty minutes later we are heading north on Rte. 15 in a brand new Ford Galaxie 500, roomy, comfortable and powerful,. The people at Hertz were delightful, even when we asked them to notify their branch office in Yuma about the Fairlane we'd left immobile down the embankment on Pine Valley Road about a mile south of Guatay. I had assured them I had taken out the insurance but just in case, they, too, received a Bowles & Bernardi business card.

We drive in silence most of the way. I'm worried about Rhonda. There's no logical reason Tootie Reese should know about the place in Escondido but he might know about the Red Sombrero and they, in turn, might have that address on her employment application. Besides, Reese and his East L.A. drug dealers aren't her only problem. The late Kurt Hogg was an emissary from Miguel Moreno and Moreno means the Mickey Cohen organization. This is a really lousy situation for a decent woman who was merely giving an old girlfriend a hand.

It's nearly eleven o'clock when I exit the freeway onto West Valley Parkway and from there to Harmony Grove. No wrong turns this time and several minutes later I am turning into Willie Scanlan's driveway. I stop twenty yards from the house, then exit the car and stand by the grill, hands raised high above my head. The Galaxie is unfamiliar to Willie and I don't want him getting frisky with his shotgun. A few moments later he emerges from the screen door, armed, of course, and peers out at me.

"Ah, the drug dealer," he says.

"That's me," I say. "How's Rhonda?"

"Not as good as she could be," he says.

I signal to Angie to join me and together we approach the house. The gun barrel is pointed at the ground. A good sign. I introduce Angie. Willie grunts in greeting.

"Shouldn't have left the hospital so soon," he says, "but she wouldn't listen. She's on the sofa watching some damned TV show. Slept a lot last night but she's still hurtin'. Been feedin' her aspirin and changed her bandage twice. Still bleeding some."

Rhonda smiles when she sees us but Willie's right. Her face is drawn and you can tell she's in pain. Maybe she's safer here than at Mercy but safety in Escondido might turn out to be fatal.

"Hiya, Joe. Nice to see you," she says.

"Same here, Rhonda," I say.

Her curious eyes flick to Angie who I introduce as my lawyer. Rhonda laughs.

"Don't look like any lawyer I know," she says."What's she doing here?"

"Helping me keep you safe."

"That'll be nice. Pops says you got the stuff stashed somewhere."

"Better where I've got it than here."

"You gonna keep it, Joe?" she smiles slyly.

"Hadn't planned to. Do more good as evidence against who-ever killed Linda."

"A hundred large is very tempting," she says.

I'm stunned. "You're saying those packages are worth a hun-dred thousand dollars?"

"Street value? Damned right."

"No wonder Tootie's so anxious to catch up with me."

"Not good, Joe," she says.

"I know. That's why I want to get us all to Yuma as soon as possible."

"What's in Yuma?" she asks.

"For you, safety. The Sheriff and the County Prosecutor want to hear your story. He's going to put you in protective custody."

"Not sure I like the sound of that. Are we talking a jail cell?"

"More likely a motel room with an armed guard."

"Sounds better."

"You feel well enough to travel?" I ask.

"As good as I'm going to," she replies.

"Then let's get to it. Willie, you coming with us?"

He shakes his head.

"Got no business in Yuma," he says.

"Suit yourself. Let's hit the road, ladies."

I cross to the door, open it and walk out onto the screened-in porch. Angie and Rhonda follow. Willie's right behind. I open the screen door and step outside. Just then a white Mustang comes wailing toward the house and skids to a stop, spraying dirt and debris in every direction. I turn back to the ladies.

"Stay on the porch," I say grimly. "I'll handle this. Willie, keep your hardware handy."

I let the screen door slam behind me as I take a couple of steps forward. Tootie gets out from behind the wheel of the Mustang and starts toward me. His jacket is open and his .38 pearl handled revolver is still jammed in his belt. He looks at me with a sadistic grin. It's my cue to be terrified. His two cohorts have exited the car and they, too, are approaching but smart enough to hang back and let Tootie run the show.

"You a big pain in the ass, you know that, man?" Tootie says smugly. He hasn't reached for his gun. Probably doesn't think he needs to.

I fall to my knees, hands at my side, starting to shake.

"Please don't hurt me," I sob.

He stops, hovering over me, then grabs a handful of shirt.

"Get up off your knees, you pussy!" he snarls, yanking me up and as he does, my right hand comes up and jams my little .25 automatic under his chin.

"You even twitch, asshole, and I blow the top of your head halfway to Tijuana." I look in his face. His eyes bulge with fear. Up close and personal, my little popgun is just as lethal as a .45 Magnum. "Now tell your boys to take their guns and throw them toward the house and you'd better pray neither of them is looking for your job."

He hesitates. I jam the gun hard into his throat.

"Coby! Jeeter! Toss your pieces away." When they hesitate, he screams at them. "You motherfuckers hear me? Toss 'em, God damn it!"

Out of the corner of my eye I can see them comply.

"Tell them to back away," I say.

"Back off!" Tootie shouts.

"Willie!" I call out. "Come on out. Bring the shotgun. Angie, call the nearest Highway Patrol barracks to come pick up this garbage."

With my free hand I pluck Tootie's pistol from his belt and back away.

"Sit down," I say to him, gun pointed directly at his privates. "Hands in your lap."

"You ain't gonna shoot me," he sneers.

"I will if I have to," I tell him.

He hesitates, then does as he's told as Willie emerges with his shotgun.

"Willie, if either of those other perverts move, blow his ass to Hell."

"Will do," Willie says with a smile in his voice.

I turn my attention back to Tootie Reese. If he is frightened or even concerned, he doesn't show it. He watches me curiously.

"What you want to bring the cops into this for?" he asks.

"Seems like a good idea. Better than letting you blow me away."

"I is sorry about that. You and me I think we can do business."

"I doubt it."

"Plenty for both of us."

"So I've been told."

"So why you want to be a hard ass, tell me that," Tootie says.

"Because a decent woman I once knew was brutally murdered and a good friend has been framed for it."

"I don't know nothin' about that," Tootie replies.

He looks away. He may be lying. I can't tell. I do know that I'm suddenly feeling very tired. He's sitting. I'm standing. What's wrong with this picture? Uncomfortable, I shift my weight. It doesn't help.

"And just what do you know, Mr. Reese?" I say, moving the pistol to my other hand.

"I know I made a deal for some high quality shit and I 'spects to get it, one way or the other."

"Tell me about your arrangement with Carlotta Moreno."

"Ain't nothin' to tell. I knows who she is and what she does so when I gets word she wants to do business. her and me we talk. She says she be ready to take ten thousand of Mickey fuckin' Cohen's money from her husband to make a buy across the border, then she sell it to me for thirty large."

"And you sell it off for a hundred thousand." My legs are getting heavy. I need to sit but I can't. Buck up, Bernardi, I say to myself. Don't let this guy smell weakness.

"That be my business, not hers. She say this be a one time deal 'cause she gonna light out and not be comin' back. I say fine, I don't care, long as I get a chance to fuck old Mickey Cohen. She supposed to call me but she doesn't so I send Jeeter to Yuma to poke around and he tells me she be dead and the way it happened, her old man caught on but what I think is, the way people is acting, nobody got the drugs. They be somewhere and then Jeeter he tells me about you and the guy the cops put in jail and I think, maybe you know where the shit is and maybe I can get it from you or maybe we make a deal, either way, so I have somebody follow you around, to San Diego and that ripoff club and the girl. You see where I'm goin'? And like I said, I didn't have fuckall to do with the girl getting killed but I want my shit and you gonna give it to me."

"I don't think so," I say.

"Five large, no questions asked."

"Not interested."

He stares at me hard and a faint smile curls his lips. My hand is wavering.

"That piece, it be gettin' heavy?"

"Maybe so," I say, "but I'll shoot you dead before I have to drop it."

"You buyin' a lot of trouble here, mister," Tootie says. "Cops arrest me and my boys, my lawyer be on the first plane to bail us out. Maybe even tonight, we be free and havin' ribs someplace and I be thinking 'bout what I'm gonna do about you, you dig? Yeah, it be nice to get that shit but even if I don't, I gotta even things up 'tween you and me, you understand? I get crap from somebody I do something about it. Elsewise my homies start lookin' at me funny."

"I'm sure they do," I say. I feel a tightness in my chest. My breathing is becoming labored.

"Ten large. That be a good deal for you, mister, and when the cops show, you just tell 'em this be a big misunderstanding."

"The only one misunderstanding around here is you, Reese. Now why don't you just shut up. I'm tired of listening to you."

"Okay. That be fine. Me and my boys, bye and bye, we'll send flowers to your lady."

I raise my eyes and look past him as two CHP cruisers, lights flashing, turn into the driveway and speed toward us. I hear the screen door slam and Angie hurries out and runs to the cop cars as four highway patrol officers exit their vehicles.

"My name is Angelique Garcia," she says. "I'm an attorney and I'm the one who called you. The three men wearing blue bandanas are gang members from East Los Angeles and they are trespassing. They also threatened Mr. Bernardi with physical harm."

"Are you the owner of the property, ma'am?" asks the lead officer who is wearing sergeant's stripes.

"That'd be me," Willie shouts out.

"And I'm Bernardi," I say helpfully.

"Well, you can lower that weapon, Mr. Bernardi. We'll take it from here. You, too, sir." he shouts out to Willie. "Shoulder your weapon. Tyler, you and Arroyo cuff those two and toss 'em in the back of your vehicle."

"Yes, sir."

Two of the troopers tend to Reese's underlings while the third is carefully looking over the Mustang. The sergeant, whose name tag reads 'Keller', leans in closer to Tootie.

"You got here fast, Sergeant," I say.

"We're close by. We got an APB on that car a couple of days ago. Been keeping a lookout." He squats down on his haunches and looks closely at Tootie. "I know this guy. We've got his picture posted on our bulletin board. Gang leader, drug dealer, something like that."

"All of the above," I say. "Name's Thomas Reese. They call him Tootie. A big shot in the Crips." I hand him Tootie's pearl handled revolver. "I took this from him. You might want to run it through ballistics. Could be a missing piece in some open case in L.A."

"Could be," Keller says, slipping the gun in his belt.

"Sarge." Keller turns as the third trooper hurries to his side carrying a small brown paper bag. "Found this in the glove compartment," he says. Keller peers inside, then reaches in and extracts several glassine envelopes filled with the kind of powder Johnson & Johnson doesn't sell at the corner Rexall. Keller looks down at Tootie.

"Selling or using, Mr. Reese?" he asks.

"Don't know nothin' about that stuff," Tootie says.

"Yeah, I'll bet," Keller says, then turns to me. "I'll need to have you folks follow me to the barracks where we can take your statements."

"We need to get to Yuma, Sergeant," I tell him. "It's important."

"Won't take long," he says. "An hour at the most."

And he was right. It was all pretty straightforward but when he asked me why I was having trouble with Reese and his boys, I ascribed it to road rage, an altercation on the freeway. I did not mention a hundred thousand dollars worth of drugs and I assumed Tootie would also remain silent on the subject. I'm not sure Keller believed me but he really had no choice.

It's now just past two 'clock and the three of us are on 80 heading east. Willie stayed behind to feed the chickens and slop the hogs. We should reach Yuma by suppertime. Tootie and his boys are locked in a holding cell, waiting for the arrival of a sleazy L.A. lawyer. Keller figures he can hold them until morning when they'll appear in court and presumably make bail. He suggests I watch my back. I suggest that he is absolutely right. With Miguel Moreno close by and Tootie possibly on the prowl, starting tomorrow morning Yuma figures to be anything but a safe haven.

# CHAPTER FOURTEEN

Last night Rhonda Scanlan and I shared quarters at the Coronado, much to the consternation of Angie Garcia who had earlier been rebuffed by me out of respect for my marital vows. No, Rhonda and I did not share a bed. She was sequestered in the room next to mine with the connecting door wide open all night and I with my pistol on my nightstand. I was bushed, so was she, and separately we slept the night away in different beds. Here's how it came about.

We arrived in Yuma around suppertime and Sheriff Dixon was absent from his premises and no one knew exactly where he was. Angie immediately suspected the good sheriff had a little action going on the side and maybe he did, but in any case, Sergeant Ramos was not about to take responsibility for Rhonda. Not my problem, he said. Check with the chief in the morning. So this is how I was finagled into booking the room next to mine at the Coronado. I didn't expect trouble but my Beretta and I were ready for it.

"You sure it's okay if I leave the door open, Rhonda," I'd said to her, lest she get the wrong idea.

"Get real," she'd replied dismissively.

"I take it you have no problem then."

"You take correctly, Joe. I'm sure many ladies consider you a stud muffin, Joe, but honestly, you're not my type. No offense."

"None taken," I'd smiled, silently wounded by such a casual dismissal of my male magnetism.

But quickly the feeling had passed and I'd consoled myself with the knowledge that, for now, I was the cop on the beat, the guy with a badge, and as I said, the night passed without incident.

Now it's morning and I go to the open connecting door and knock loudly.

"Are you decent?" I call in without peeking.

"I try to be," Rhonda calls back, "but I don't always succeed."

I look in. She's sitting at a vanity applying mascara and looking very attractive in a plaid skirt and a navy blue cotton sweater. She looks at me in the mirror.

"Are we expected?" she asks.

"Ten o'clock. I just got off the phone with Sergeant Ramos. How are you feeling?"

"Better," she says. "Bleeding's stopped. You?"

"I slept well," I say.

"I know. I heard you," she smiles and gets up from the vanity. "Time for breakfast?"

"Barely," I say, checking my watch. It's then that I notice the empty whiskey miniature on the vanity, halfway concealed by a Kleenex box. I crane my neck and peek into the trash basket. Four more empties. Two scotch, one vodka, one gin. Either she has eclectic taste or she indiscriminately used up whatever they had stocked. I lean toward the latter

She has wandered into my room, looking around admiringly. I join her.

"You have a bigger sofa than I do."

"I have pull with management," I say as I go into the bathroom and close the door. The first thing I do is draw a glass of water from the tap and retrieve a couple of aspirin from my travel kit. When

138

I told Rhonda I was feeling better, I didn't mean I felt good. I have aches and pains from scalp to toenails. The effects of my ordeal continue to linger within my 45 year old body and if I were smart I'd drop out for a couple of days to recuperate. But I'm not smart and I can't afford a couple of days so I will try to muddle along without complaint. I'm in the midst of expelling the remnants of last night's Dos Equiis when I hear the phone ring twice, then Rhonda's muffled voice. By the time I emerge from the bathroom, she's hung up.

"Who was on the phone?" I ask.

"Your wife," she replies.

Wonderful, I think to myself. A woman in my hotel room at nine in the morning at the precise moment Bunny decides to call.

"She thought I was a lawyer," Rhonda says. "I told her I wasn't, that Angelique was the lawyer. I was just a good friend."

Good friend, I think. Yeah, that'll go over well.

"You should have called me to the phone," I say.

"I offered but she wasn't interested. She said to tell you that a call later today would be nice if you can spare the time."

"And what did you say?"

"I didn't. That's when she hung up on me. I think she was annoyed."

I grab the phone and dial out. It rings four times before it is answered by a female voice.

"Bernardi residence," says Bridget O'Shaugnessy.

"It's me, Bridget. Is she there?"

"Herself is just after leavin' for work, sir, where she'd prefer you didn't call her. Her words, sir. Not mine."

So much for the third thing of which my dear wife is totally sure. My fidelity.

"All right, if she phones home, tell her I'll call her this evening."

"Oh, I wouldn't wait that long, sir."

"What are you talking about, Bridget?"

139

"It's been my observation, sir, that in a situation like this, the missus will begin to regret her behavior at the end of the first hour. At the end of hour two, she will worry that she has acted childishly and by hour three, she will be frantic with remorse. May I suggest a call to her office at noon?"

"You may, Bridget, and thank you."

"Not necessary, sir. It's my job to shelter the little one from her hardheaded argumentative parents." She hangs up.

I think to myself, what would we ever do without this wonderfully loving and irreplaceable woman?

Rhonda looks at me hopefully. "Breakfast?"

I check my watch again and then shake my head solemnly.

"No time," I say.

It's now ten o'clock and we are gathered in the Sheriff's office. Me, Rhonda and Angie representing the good guys. Joshua Dixon and a beady-eyed bureaucrat named Foster Willoughby, the county attorney, for the opposition. Willoughby exudes suspicion each time any of us speaks but in the end Rhonda's narrative forces him to face the reality of Army McLeod's innocence. By eleven o'clock Army has been released into Angie's custody. As for Rhonda, one of Dixon's deputies quit to work security at the airport and a second has come down with a bad case of shingles making it impossible for Dixon to provide Rhonda with protection. After much back and forth I find myself stuck with the job for at least one more night but no more. Tomorrow, after handing Sheriff Dixon the remote opener to the storage locker in Escondido, I travel back to L.A. into the arms of my wife and daughter. With Army cleared of Linda's death, I have no good reason to stick around and as for Rhonda's safety, I'll pass that responsibility on to Army. He owes her that much and frankly, I'm sick of the whole situation.

Freed from incarceration, Army gives me a huge embrace of gratitude and then shyly shakes hands with the ladies. His joy fades when he looks in the Sheriff's direction.

"No hard feelings, Sheriff, but you and I both know who is responsible."

"I'm not sure about that, Mr. McLeod. In any case, knowing and proving it are two different matters."

"I'm just telling you, do something about Miguel Moreno or I will."

Dixon's eyes narrow.

"Meaning?" he asks.

I jump in hurriedly. Army has a talent for saying the wrong thing to the wrong person at the wrong time.

"Okay, Army, that's enough."

"I'm just telling him—-"

"We all heard what you were telling him and I'm telling you to shut the hell up."

At that moment, Rhonda very vociferously insists we go in search of breakfast and a few minutes later the four of us are walking in the door of a nearby Howard Johnson. Army, who has been subsisting on watery Cream of Wheat, weak lukewarm coffee and dry toast, now orders eggs, waffles, bacon, sausage and a carafe of extra strong French blend. Halfway through the meal, he begins to muse about dinner.

For almost an hour, our spirits are high and we banter with one another but I'm very aware of an undercurrent of tension that puts the lie to our forced gaiety. Linda is still quite dead, her body lying in the morgue awaiting a court ordered autopsy. Several times I look over at Army and the smile is there, forced and frozen like a swath of paint across his face. Angie sees it too. Not only has Army lost the love of his life but he knows, as do we all, that Tootie Reese is not done with us. Neither is Miguel Moreno. If I were a better citizen I'd see this through to its conclusion but I've had enough of this tawdry business. My body continues to rebel in a hundred different ways from bruises to pulled muscles and my acutely intelligent brain keeps telling me if I continue to involve myself in this adventure, only bad things will ensue. No, this is no longer my affair.

Following brunch, Angie returns to her office taking Rhonda with her. I phone Bunny at the newspaper and she quickly accepts my perfectly rational explanation of why a woman was in my hotel room at nine o'clock in the morning. She reiterates that she trusts me implicitly. I suspect that this rock solid belief in my monogamy will last until the next time a woman answers the phone in my hotel room. Following this chat I drive Army out to the location in the desert. Initially, Army is silent, deep in thought. Finally he speaks.

"You know, Linda was your friend as well as mine."

"I know that."

"Look, Joe, I don't want you to think I'm ungrateful. You've saved my ass and I won't soon forget it, but I don't understand how you can just walk away when Linda's killer is running around free."

"That's Dixon's job, Army. Not mine. Not yours."

"You expect a lot from that bigoted bastard," Army says bitterly.

"I have no choice, old friend. I owe it to Bunny and Yvette to keep myself in one piece. I'm no longer a thirty-year-old Don Quixote as my doctor so eloquently told me a short while ago."

He looks at me, frowning.

"What's wrong, Joe?" he asks with genuine concern.

"Nothing terminal, not yet. Just a whole lot of little things that need tending to."

"Sorry. I didn't know."

"How could you?" I say. "Word of advice, Army. Concentrate on your job and avoid Miguel Moreno. To Linda, he was nothing more than a safe haven no matter what he may claim to the contrary."

"Did he kill her, Joe?"

I glance in Army's direction. He's staring straight ahead, his visage grim.

"I don't know," I say. "If he did the law will catch up with him. If he didn't and you do something foolish, you'll have destroyed the rest of your life."

He looks over at me with a sad expression.

"What life is that, Joe?" he asks.

Cast and crew alike are delighted to have Army once again in their midst which apparently doesn't say much for my contributions in his absence. The lunch break is half over but that doesn't stop Army from grabbing four soft tacos and a side of linguini to scarf down on top of his Howard Johnson repast. Me, I settle for a soda and a piece of danish as we answer questions. Army's arrest was a big misunderstanding, I tell them. There are no suspects and the Sheriff is following up on several viable leads, the latter being a bald-faced lie since Dixon has no clue as to how to proceed.

Several times I catch Miguel Moreno watching me and I wonder how much he knows about our run in with Tootie Reese and his fellow Crips. Probably a lot. I doubt that the Cohen organization grew to be wealthy and powerful by remaining ignorant of the world around them. I look for some sign of Marcus Bloom, the newly arrived muscle. There is none so he's either working the cantina in town or he's returned to Los Angeles.

After lunch I say my goodbyes to my newly made acquaintances. They are polite enough to say they're sorry to see me go and I'm sure they mean it as far as it goes. The film industry is one that doesn't boast a great deal of sentimentality and with tens of thousands of talented people on the outside looking in, watching out for number one is a priority if you wish to survive. Twas ever thus from the first cowboy to hit town from Helena, Montana, determined to unseat William S. Hart from his perch atop the pyramid.

I head for the parking area and I spot him immediately, leaning against my rented Galaxie. I thought Miguel Moreno and I had concluded our business at the prison museum but apparently not.

"You've been busy," he says to me as I reach the car.

"Have I?"

"Word gets around. You know, Joe, as long as you have the goods in your possession, Reese isn't going to leave you alone."

"I've thought of that. That's why I'm I'm turning everything over to Sheriff Dixon tomorrow just before I head back to Los Angeles."

"Foolish, Joe. Very foolish. My offer still stands."

"You know, Moreno, if you were so damned desperate to get hold of the drugs, you probably shouldn't have killed your wife before she gave them up."

His eyes narrow into cold slits of anger.

"I didn't kill her and when I find the bastard that did, I'm going to slit his throat."

"You should save that thought for someone who might be tempted to believe it," I say.

"I don't care if you believe me or not. She's the only good thing that ever happened to me. I would never have harmed her."

"She didn't love you, you know."

"I knew that. It didn't matter. I was important to her. She needed me. That was enough."

"And then she betrayed you."

"That's right. I thought I'd done something to alienate her. Later I learned that an old boyfriend had come back into her life. Him I could have killed if I believed in killing which I don't. My associates, they are another breed of animal."

"A well known fact."

"If you retain possession of the goods, they will come after you, Joe. So will Reese. The only question is who gets to you first."

"Like I said, Moreno. Tomorrow the drugs will be in the hands of the Sheriff."

"Be sure to get a receipt."

"What's that supposed to mean?"

"It means that at times Sheriff Dixon is approachable, especially where tens of thousands of dollars are involved. Before he was elected Sheriff, he ran a barely successful private security firm. Rumors flew about how Dixon did business but nothing was proved. It would be a shame if Reese and his boys were to grab you for the drugs when you no longer had them your possession, beat the crap out of you or worse and Dixon had them stashed somewhere, playing deaf, dumb and blind."

"I doubt he'd do that," I say.

"Then you're worse than naive, you're stupid. Look, Joe, I'm going to level with you. I'm in a bind. My associates—-"

"The ones from L.A.—"

"That's right. They are holding me responsible for my wife's treachery, even though I knew nothing about it. If I can't produce the drugs within the next couple of days, well, Marcus Bloom is here to be certain I do and if I don't, he has his orders. I don't have to tell you what they are."

"I get the picture."

"That ten thousand I offered you, that's coming out of my own pocket."

I shrug. "Every enterprise has a certain amount of overhead."

His face contorts in rage.

"This is no Goddamned joke, Bernardi. These people are fucking serious. You go to the Sheriff and I'm a dead man."

"A little late to worry about that now, Moreno. What's the old cliche? You lie down with dogs, you get up with fleas. Maybe you should have thought of that before you jabbed her with cigarette burns all over her body and pressed a pistol to the back of her head—"

"I told you, I didn't kill her!" he screams and immediately looks around to see if he's been overheard. "Twenty five thousand, it's all

I have in ready cash. I can't make it more."

"For the last time, Moreno, I'm not interested. If you think the Sheriff can be easily bought, deal with him."

He starts to say something, then thinks better of it. He stares at me hard, then speaks quietly. "Twenty-five thousand dollars tax free, Joe. Think about it. Think about it hard. If you change your mind, I'll be at the cantina this evening. We close at ten, I'll stay until eleven o'clock. Remember this. Cash is only one means of persuasion. There are others, infinitely less pleasant."

"Don't threaten me, Moreno," I warn him,

"Then don't dick with me. No later than eleven," he repeats, then brushes past me, headed toward his catering truck. I'm still grappling with his indictment of the Sheriff's integrity. I have no use for Dixon. He's surly and bigoted and a bully and in that way a disgrace to his badge but I've had no reason to question his honesty. I'm also pretty sure that Angie would have mentioned it, even if it were merely unprovable gossip.

I hop into the car and start the drive into town. A couple of things are troubling me. Twice Moreno denied killing Linda. I read people pretty well and my gut tells me he may be telling the truth. If so, that turns everything upside down. I had planned to call the airlines before supper but it looks like I may have to rethink that. My new priority is a chat with Angie Garcia to learn just how much she really knows about Joshua Dixon.

As soon as I get back to the hotel, I phone Bunny at her office at the newspaper. She pretends to be annoyed but I see through her. She asks how it's going and I say lousy. She asks when I'm coming home and I tell her maybe tomorrow. I can hear her brighten. Then, when things are just about perfect, she asks who is Dr. McCaffrey? I've been sandbagged. I am momentarily mute.

"Joe?"

"Yes?"

"Who is Dr. McCaffrey?"

"Who?"

"Dr. McCaffrey."

"Oh, that guy,.." I say with a chuckle.

"Yes, that guy. He wants to see you in his office at three o'clock Friday afternoon."

"Right. I'll call him."

"Joe, who is he?"

"Lev Rosen referred me to him."

"Yes, but who is he?"

"He's—he's a very high priced nutritionist. That twenty pounds I have to lose, it's more like thirty and McCaffrey's going to help me do it."

"More chicken," Bunny says.

"Oh, yes, lots more."

"And lots of green vegetables."

"That, too," I say.

"I'll alert Bridget so she can start planning some recipes."

"Wonderful idea," I say.

"Then we'll see you tomorrow evening for dinner?"

"That's the plan."

"Can't wait."

"Me, either."

"Love you."

"Same here."

I make a little kissy noise into the phone and hang up, groaning audibly. Chicken and green vegetables for the rest of my life. Suicide briefly comes to mind. With a sigh I pick up the phone again and dial Angie at her office. Angie's gal Friday, Myrna Love, answers and puts me right through. Rhonda is safely with her, out in the foyer reading a movie magazine but she is antsy, Angie tells me, and clearly unhappy. She wants to get back to San Diego but with

Tootie Reese on the loose, she knows she can't. Angie hints strongly that I should come to her office and take custody of Rhonda. I say I will but not right away and then I ask her about Miguel Moreno's assertion that Sheriff Dixon is for sale. She denies it. Like me she has no use for the man but there has never been any question about his honesty. In her opinion Moreno is playing with my head. I thank her and promise to come by no later than five to pick up Rhonda. "Five???" I hear her wail just as I hang up and lay back on the bed, leaving the phone off the cradle.

I have been feeling like crap ever since I got up this morning. I feel a lump in my chest which could be gas or something more serious, I don't know. I do know that the least exertion is causing me to lose my breath and I am positive this is not a good sign. Maybe I should see a doctor but what's he going to tell me? Things I already know? Send me off to a hospital for tests I have already taken? A few hours sleep, that's all I need, I tell myself, as I close my eyes and my brain starts to shut down. No question, a few hours sleep and I'll be as good as new.

# CHAPTER FIFTEEN

I have an alarm clock in my head. It's always been with me, even when I was a kid, and it's never failed me which is why, at quarter to five, I sit bolt upright in the bed and check the clock on the nightstand. As anticipated, it reads quarter to five. I slip off the bed, trudge into the bathroom where I splash cold water all over my face, and meticulously comb what's left of my once thick black hair. I pick up the phone and dial Army's room. No answer. Still filming, no doubt. I dial the parking valet and ask him to bring the car around front, then head for the elevator. There is something of a spring in my step and the lump in my chest has gone away. Silently I warn myself to stop looking for trouble. I could be in danger of turning into a full blown hypochondriac.

The elevator doors open and I step out into the lobby. The first thing I see is Jimmy Stewart near the entrance chatting with an elderly couple. They share a laugh and then the couple heads out and Stewart strides toward the registration desk. I intercept him halfway there.

"Jim!"

"Oh, hi, Joe," Stewart says. "Where have you been keeping yourself?"

"It's a long story. You broke early today."

"A sand storm whipped up and disabled the camera," he says as we reach the desk.

"What about the backup?"

"That was the backup. Lost the first one a few days back. Darned sand just keeps gumming things up. They're flying a new one down from the studio. Should have it first thing in the morning."

"Have you seen Army McLeod? I tried his room. He's not there."

"I'm pretty sure I saw him get on the crew bus. Maybe thirty minutes ago. Could have stopped off for a couple of brews with some of the boys."

"Yeah, that's probably it," I say. "If you see him, would you tell him I'm looking for him."

"Sure thing," Stewart says as he turns to the desk clerk to get his room key.

Angelique Garcia, Attorney at Law, maintains an office in a small building near city hall. I drive up to it six minutes later, feed the meter and hurry inside. Almost immediately, I know something is wrong. I open the door to Angie's reception area and find it empty, then hear loud female voices coming from a private office in the rear. When I poke my head in I discover Angie toe-to-toe in a shouting match with a Rubenesque young lady who I take to be her faithful gal Friday, Myrna Love. Rhonda Scanlan is nowhere in sight. It seems Myrna was in need of a potty break down the corridor and once left on her own, Rhonda split for places unknown.

"Joe, I am so sorry," Angie says. "My fault."

"No, mine," Myrna says. "Stupid and careless."

"Apparently so," I say, "but done is done. Have either of you any idea where she might have gone?"

"About an hour ago she asked me where the nearest bar was," Myrna says.

"And?"

"And what?"

"And where?"

"Right across the street. Toby's Top Hat."

"I'll take a look," I say. "Angie, call the Sheriff, have his people keep an eye out for her. And by the way, have you heard from Army?"

"No, should I have?" she asks.

"Maybe not. The film has wrapped for the day but he's not in his hotel room."

"Foul play?"

"Let's hope not," I say. "Stick here by the phone while I try to find Rhonda."

Rhonda's not at Toby's Top Hat. I know because the CLOSED sign is hanging in the front door right above a little cardboard clock which indicates they will open at five o'clock. I look around, spot two likely watering holes a couple of blocks away and hoof it. They are both open but no Rhonda. I realize I've made a terrible mistake. It's obvious now that Rhonda has "the Irish disease" even though I doubt she'd admit to it but beyond that, she should have been immediately placed under lock and key for her own safety. Yuma is no Phoenix but neither is it a one-horse desert crossroads. Finding her is going to be difficult, especially if she doesn't want to be found, and I have no idea where to start.

By seven o'clock the Sheriff's Department is keeping an eye out for her and I have personally checked out 22 bars within six blocks in all directions of Angie's office building. No sign of Rhonda at any of them which I find odd. A drunk in search of booze will zero in on the closest available source. Guaranteed.

By seven thirty Angie and I are tired and hungry and in her office devouring several cartons of Chinese food, waiting by the phone in case we hear from either Army or Rhonda. The hotel clerk has this number should either return to the Coronado. Myrna would have joined us for the moo goo gai pan but received a phone call from her building superintendent that a flamboyantly dressed street-walker was camped out by Myrna's apartment door claiming to be her mother. A quick description confirmed the fact and a furious Myrna left to tend to family business.

Angie and I chat for a while over the food but we are both tense and worried. Conversation comes hard. Rhonda is gone of her own volition. Army is missing under circumstances we can only guess at and those guesses are not pretty to contemplate. By ten o'clock Angie has had enough and so have I. She heads for home and a warm bed while I start to drive toward the Coronado. I'm halfway there when I remember Miguel Moreno's invitation. He wants to do business. I need information about the whereabouts of my friends. He might know something or he might not. Anyway, it's worth a shot.

I make a turn onto E. 32nd Street and head west. As I recall the cantina is on the left hand side across from a Texaco station. I spot it, darkened, a couple of security lights on inside, the parking area is deserted except for a late model Pontiac parked by the end of the building. I turn in off the street, my headlights playing on the entrance just as the door flies open and a figure emerges, running. I recognize him immediately and slam on the brakes, then leap from the car.

"Army! Wait!" I call out.

He stops and turns toward me, his face contorted in panic. He hurries in my direction.

"Joe! Jesus, it's awful. I just wanted to talk to him, I swear to God, just talk."

Now I get a better look. His shirt is covered with something dark that could easily be blood.

"What are you talking about?"

"Moreno. Inside. On the kitchen floor. I didn't do it, Joe. I found him that way."

152

I slide past him and hurry into the cantina, dimly illuminated by a couple of work lights. Army is hard on my heels and leads me to the double swinging doors at the rear of the room. He pushes through into the kitchen, flipping on the lights, me on his heels. I see him right away, flat on his back, his torso drenched with blood and a blood soaked hunting knife lying on the floor a couple of feet away. Moreno's eyes are wide open, his face frozen in an expression of disbelief. I kneel down beside him but searching for a pulse would be a waste of time. Miguel Moreno is very, very dead.

"I pulled the knife from his chest, Joe, and tried to give him artificial respiration. But he was dead, even though his body was still warm."

"Stupid, Army. Really stupid," I say. "You got your fingerprints all over the bloody knife and blood all over your shirt."

"I know. I wasn't thinking."

"What are you doing here, Army?"

"I—uh—I wanted to ask him some questions. About Linda, I mean."

"Just talk."

"That's right, just talk."

"And did you bring the knife with you, Army? It doesn't look like a kitchen knife."

"I never saw it before, Joe. I told you what happened."

"Yes, I heard you. I'm not sure I believe you."

Just then I hear a car pull up outside. I get to my feet and go into the dining room, then peer outside. Two cruisers, lights flashing, have just pulled up outside. A few moments later, Sergeant Ramos enters followed by two of his deputies.

"In here," I say to him and step aside as he walks into the kitchen. He glances at the body and then takes in Army and his blood stained shirt.

"Can't let you out of our sight, can we, Mr. McLeod?" Ramos

sneers.

"I didn't do this," Army says.

"Then what are you doing here?"

Army repeats the same half-baked story he gave me and it's obvious Ramos isn't buying it.

"Holly, cuff this gentleman and you and Perez take him to head-quarters——"

"Now wait a minute——"

"—and if he gives you any trouble, do what you have to do to gain his cooperation. Notify forensics, then call the coroner and tell him to get his ass over here, chop,chop."

"Yes, sir, " the deputy says as he grabs Army and spins him around, cuffing first one wrist, then the other. They start out.

"Joe, call Angelique!" Army calls to me over his shoulder.

"I will!" I shout.

Perez hustles Army out the door to one of the cruisers, all the while Army protesting his innocence.

Ramos stares down at the body. I stare at Ramos.

"So, Sergeant, what brings you here at this time of night?" I ask casually.

"A phone call."

"From who?"

"No idea."

"Anonymous?"

"Yes."

"Good old Anonymous," I say. "He gets around. You took the call?"

"Yes."

"It was a he."

"That's right."

"Recognize the voice?"

"No."

"I have an idea who might be responsible for this," I say.

"That so?"

"An associate of Moreno's from Los Angeles. His name is Marcus Bloom. Moreno was definitely afraid of him."

"I know Bloom," Ramos says. "He didn't do it."

"Are you sure?"

"Two of my men helped Bloom onto a plane first thing this morning."

"On what grounds?" I ask.

"I don't need grounds, Bernardi. This is Arizona, not California. Having people like Bloom hanging around gives Yuma a bad name. We're also keeping an eye out for Tootie Reese. Same reason."

"Law and order seems to flourish here, Sergeant."

"We try."

"Incidentally, you got here quickly, Sergeant. Mr. McLeod says when he tried resuscitation the body was still very warm."

"And your point is?"

"An observation, that's all."

"I will tell you what I observe, Mr. Bernardi. When I asked McLeod what he was doing here, he did not have a satisfactory answer. I think perhaps down at the station house, I'll get one."

"That sounds ominous. Where's your interrogation room, in the basement?" I walk over to a nearby wall where a telephone is mounted, "I'd better call his lawyer and let her know what's going on."

"Time enough for that later, Bernardi," Ramos says sharply. "How about if you tell me what brought you here this time of night."

"I was invited by Mr. Moreno. He had business he wanted to discuss where we wouldn't risk being overheard."

"The drugs," Ramos says.

"You know about that."

"Of course I do. The chief told me."

He reaches in his shirt pocket and takes out a small cigarillo. He lights up. The fumes remind me of a poorly maintained stable.

"You're a brave guy, Bernardi, hanging on to that stuff," he says with a smile. "You've got a target painted on your back but you don't seem to care."

"Nothing's going to happen to me as long as I have the drugs and no one but me knows where they are."

"No doubt the lady felt the same way before they started poking her with lit cigarettes. If I were you I would seriously consider turning those drugs over to us for safe keeping."

"The Sheriff doesn't see it that way."

"The Sheriff doesn't always make wise choices," Ramos says. "In fact his main talent is electioneering. He is smart enough to know that and leaves actual law enforcement to others."

"Like you."

"That's right. I really think it would be wise of you and certainly safer if you were to tell me where you have stashed the drugs."

"I appreciate your concern, Sergeant," I say with a smile, "but I think I'll leave things the way they are, at least for the present."

There had been a trace of geniality in his expression but now it fades, replaced by a steely glare. In the distance I hear the wail of an ambulance drawing near. Ramos hears it, too.

"Keep my offer in mind, Mr. Bernardi. The drugs will be safe and so will you."

# CHAPTER SIXTEEN

Midnight. The witching hour. At the Sheriff's headquarters in Yuma, the scene is bedlam. Angelique Garcia has just walked in, demanding to see her client who is being held in a small cell in the rear of the building. Sergeant Ramos has no intention of making him available, at least not until he has taken a full statement of Army's activities, vis a vis the dead Miguel Moreno. Sheriff Dixon has decided to remain at his small two-bedroom bachelor pad on the outskirts of the town, allowing Ramos to handle this crisis on his own. I overheard two deputies discussing this situation and the name of a young school teacher called Dolly Thatcher popped into the conversation. Apparently there are times when Joshua Dixon must not, under any circumstances, be summoned from his home and this appears to be one of them.

As for me I am sitting on a visitor's bench sipping a warm can of soda which I just bought from a vending machine and watching the scene with minimal interest. Truth be told, I am exhausted and want nothing more than to return to the hotel and get a good night's sleep. Ramos has not given me permission to leave. On the other hand neither has he ordered me to stay. I consider my options, then toss away the empty soda can and casually edge my way toward the front entrance. I'm about a foot away from freedom when the door bursts open and two deputies enter. Between them they are half-carrying, half-dragging Rhonda Scanlan whose hair is tangled mess, makeup smeared and eyes so bleary I'm surprised she can see at all. She smiles at me and manages to slur something that sounds a lot like 'Hiya, Joe'.

Ramos takes one look and orders her cuffed to the visitor's bench until he can get around to her, preoccupied as he is with the legalistic threats being hurled at him by Angie Garcia. I do an about face and sit down next to Rhonda who is holding her head in her free hand.

"Where have you been?" I ask quietly. She just shakes her head. "You smell like a backwoods still."

"Not surprised," she mutters.

She's leaning so far forward she's in danger of pitching onto the floor, possibly breaking her cuffed wrist in the process. I grab her by her hair and pull her back to a sitting position.

"Screw you, Joe," she says looking away from me. She'd kept it pretty well hidden but now the real Rhonda Scanlan has put in an appearance. "Fuckin' son of a bitch."

"Thanks," I say.

"No, not you, Joe. Never you. Miguel fucking Moreno, that's who I'm talkin' about. Fuckin' son of a bitch."

"What about him?"

"Killed Linda. Son of a bitch."

"How do you know, Rhonda? He tell you that?"

"Didn't have to. Bought a knife. Gonna cut his fuckin' heart out." She digs in her windbreaker pocket, frowns then starts to look in the pockets of her blue jeans. "Where's my knife? Somebody stole my fucking knife."

"What kind of knife was it, Rhonda?"

"Sharp." She continues to rummage through her pockets, "My wallet. The bastards got my wallet, too. All my money." She holds up her free hand and peers at her bare wrist. "And my watch.

Miserable pricks."

"Rhonda, try to be quiet about your knife," I say. "Would you like a soda? I'll get you a soda. Just sit still and keep your mouth shut."

I get up and cross the room to the vending machine. One of the deputies who brought her in has just bought a warm ginger ale.

"What's the story?" I ask him, head nodding in Rhonda's direction.

"My partner and me found her sleeping it off on a bench in Gateway Park," he says. "She's had a snootful."

"I can tell. She say anything, I mean about where she's been and what she's been doing?"

"Nope. Just kept talking to herself, over and over. Beautiful Linda, that's what she kept saying. Beautiful Linda."

"Alcohol level?"

"Through the roof. Took two of us to administer the breathalyzer. She couldn't even stand."

I shake my head and look over at her, the most miserable example of womanhood I have ever seen and it's at that moment that I realize I have been missing a significant piece of this puzzle. She and Linda were friends. But suppose they were more than friends or, at the very least, Rhonda wanted it that way. I think back to her description of her encounter with her boss and her threat to use a box cutter on his manhood. I also remember her telling me quite emphatically that I wasn't her type and now I think I know why. I buy a 7up and bring it back to her. She grabs it gratefully and takes a deep swig.

"So what did Miguel have to say for himself?" I ask in a whisper.

"Nothin'," she says. "Too damned busy. Back and forth, back and forth. In the kitchen, in the dining room. Figured I'd come back later. Needed a drink."

"And when you came back later?"

"Don't know. Don't remember."

"You don't remember stabbing him?"

She looks at me and starts to giggle.

"Did I? Good for me. How is he?"

"Dead."

"Even better."

I lean in close to her and speak quietly.

"Rhonda, I don't think you should say anything right now. If the sergeant asks you something, remain silent."

"I'd rather celebrate," she mutters.

I look up as Ramos heads toward the back of the building, apparently to talk to Army. I wave at Angie, beckoning her. She starts toward me. I get up and meet her halfway.

"What's with Rhonda?" she asks.

"She needs a lawyer real bad," I say.

"Better yet, a cold shower."

"That,too," I say.

"Can't help her, Joe. I've got a client."

"She may have done Miquel."

Angie grimaces.

"Still can't help her. Conflict of interest. Look, Joe, tell her to keep quiet, say nothing."

"Did that but she's still plastered."

"I can get her somebody tomorrow morning but not now."

"I understand. Look, Angie, I'm totally washed out. That lump in my chest is coming back. I need to get out of here and get back to my bed and get some sleep."

She nods.

"Okay. Do what you have to do. Leave her to me."

"You sure?"

"I can tap dance until dawn. Go."

I nod and head for the door. Without Ramos to stop me I make it into the cool night air. My head starts to clear but I still feel lousy. I find my car and drive away. Twenty minutes later I'm sliding under the covers of my bed at the Coronado and after taking the phone off the cradle the last thing I do is repeat to myself several times, 'Noon. Noon. Noon.' Then I close my eyes and feel myself falling into a deep dark chasm.

I climb out of the chasm at two minutes to twelve. Because I forgot to pull the curtains last night, my room is bright and cheery. I am not. I want nothing more than to fly away home but I know I can't. Two friends are in deep trouble and one of them may be a killer. I swing my legs off the bed and belch. I've been doing that a lot lately and I have more or less convinced myself that the heaviness in my chest is gas. I'm not equipped emotionally to face the alternative so I pop a Tums from the bottle on my night table, wondering how long I can delay calling Bunny to tell her I won't be coming home, at least not today. I replace the handset back on the phone cradle and immediately, the little red message light starts to blink. Screw it. It'll keep until after I've showered.

I should have showered longer. When I finally retrieve my message it's from Angie who tells me to get down to her office right away. I'm not used to taking orders from dames, particularly ones I've only known for days. She can keep. I have other calls to make. I call home, knowing Bunny won't be there, and tell Bridget to tell Bunny that I won't be returning home this evening. Not the bravest thing I've ever done but it precludes another possible conversation about Dr. McCaffrey, my so-called 'diet doctor'. Then I put in a call to my old friend Mick Clausen, L.A.'s premier bail bondsman and current husband of my first wife.

"I need help," I tell him when he comes on the phone.

"Of course you do," Mick says. "You always need help. What is it this time, Joe? You need bail money? Are you being held for ransom? If it's more than five hundred bucks I won't pay."

"Weren't you once some kind of detective?" I ask.

"Actually I was a very fine detective but that was eons ago, my friend. Now what the hell do you need a detective for?"

"I need to know the life story of a Sergeant in the Yuma Sheriff's Department. Name Hector Ramos. I need everything you can get on him."

"And you need this why?"

"I need to know if I can trust him. If I miscalculate, I may never leave Yuma alive."

I explain my situation which, in the telling, sounds a lot worse than it is. I think. As usual Mick is alarmed by my foolhardiness but he knows he isn't going to talk me out of anything. He promises to see what he can find out and says he'll call me at the hotel around six with whatever he is able to dig up.

I wander into Angie's office around one-fifteen carrying a small paper bag in which there is a hardboiled egg, a cheese danish and a container of hot black coffee. Call it breakfast or brunch, I call it 'not much', but I was in no mood to sit around the coffee shop at a table for one for an hour I cannot spare. Myrna Love is sitting at the reception desk. An older and not quite as attractive version of Myrna is sitting on a small sofa. She's wearing lots of bangles, a short skirt, knee high boots and enough makeup to supply the Radio City Rockettes. As soon as she sees me, she throws me a come hither smile and a sultry 'Good morning, good lookin'.

"Knock it off, Ma," Myrna growls.

"Just being friendly," Ma protests.

"Read your magazine and be quiet," Myrna says, then looks at me and nods toward the door to Angie's private office. "She's expecting you."

I nod and go in. Angie is sitting behind her desk totally absorbed in some paperwork. I sit in the chair opposite her, open my paper bag and extract my food, then crack my egg on the side of her pencil caddy. I start peeling away eggshell and depositing same back into the bag.

"I like the way you rushed over here," she says without looking up.

"I overslept,"I say.

"I was forced to deny myself that luxury." she says and then putting down her pencil on top of her paperwork, she looks me in the eye. "You'll be happy to know that Rhonda Scanlan didn't murder anyone."

"Great news," I say, taking a big bite of egg and washing it down with coffee.

"In the alley behind some burger joint, they picked up an unwashed bum using two big plastic garbage bags for a waterbed. He had Rhonda's wallet in his pocket along with her watch and an ugly looking switchblade knife she had bought from a pawn shop yesterday afternoon."

"So they let her go."

"They're holding her on a charge of public drunkenness and vagrancy. A colleague, Teddy Frost, is pretty sure he'll have her out by suppertime but Ramos is being squirrley about her. He now has a second dead body on his hands and if he could he'd arrest the entire population of Yuma just to be sure he'd covered all bases."

"And the Sheriff?"

"He held a press conference outside his headquarters at ten this morning assuring the populace that everything was being done to bring the killer of Miguel Moreno to justice. He doesn't have a clue either. In attendance were a reporter from the Yuma Morning Sun and on-air correspondents from Yuma's two television outlets."

"And Army?"

"He's facing arraignment first thing tomorrow morning."

"What the hell's the matter with that county prosecutor? Army didn't kill anyone. He must be nuts."

163

Angie nods sagely.

"Yeah, it's hard to figure where he's coming from, Army with all that blood on his shirt and his prints on the bloody knife, not to mention the fact that a couple of days ago he threatened to kill the guy. In front of the Sheriff, no less."

"Are you still on board, Angie?" I ask.

"Of course I am, Joe. I don't walk away when things get tough." She puts emphasis on the 'I', assuming I'm going to run for it.

"Ouch," I say.

"When's your flight?" she asks.

"I haven't booked yet."

"West Coast Airlines Flight 65 to L.A. leaves at 3:55. Last plane out. You don't want to miss it."

"Thanks for the tip," I say.

"Think nothing of it," Angie says. "Anything else? No? Then I guess you can leave."

"Yeah," I say. "Thanks for everything, Ang."

"It's what they pay me for," she replies turning her attention back to her paperwork.

I go to the door and then I turn back.

"I suppose if I missed that 3:55 it wouldn't matter much."

"Probably not."

"Don't know how much use I'd be staying."

"If Army is innocent," she says, "and let's start with that premise and if Marcus Bloom left Yuma long before the killing, which he did - I checked- and Rhonda is also in the clear, which she is, that means the guilty party is running around free. Assuming that Tootie Reese didn't sneak into town unobserved and I doubt that he did, that leaves two glaring avenues of exploration, both of which involve the movie company filming at the edge of the city."

"How do you figure that?"

"One possibility is Luigi and his wife who now own the cantina and the catering business outright. I find this pretty farfetched. I've met the two of them. They are good people. Second possibility. Didn't you tell me that the Cohen operation has somebody planted on the crew undercover?"

"I was told it was likely."

"Well, somebody needs to dig around out there and the only one I know with free access to the film set is you, Joe. I'm sure Army would be very grateful for anything you could learn but of course, maybe I'm expecting too much in the way of loyalty to an old friend."

I nod. I've been politely skewered and there's no way around it.

"Well, for the record I've already notified my wife I won't be coming home this evening."

"Of course you have," Angie says.

"Yes, I have."

"Who's arguing?"

"I just want it on the record," I say.

"Fine," she says. "When I find a record to put it on, I'll do so."

"All I'm saying is, what difference is another day going to make?"

Angie smiles.

"My thoughts exactly."

Peeved, I stride to the door, then turn back to her.

"Just for my own information, Angelique, how many men have divorced you? So far, I mean."

She looks up smiling.

"See you later, Joe."

# CHAPTER SEVENTEEN

If you want to know who's who on a movie set, the guy to see is the assistant director. The Director is the commanding officer, the a.d. is the top sergeant who eats, lives and sweats with the crew. In many cases he had a lot to do with them being hired. No a.d. wants his operation screwed up by some lens puller or dolly grip he's never worked with before. On most sets, if I wanted the straight skinny, I'd get it from the a.d. but on this film, Cliff Coleman is young and new to the game. I think this may be only his second or third as a First. Nonetheless I approach him anyway. There are 65 men and women working the picture and I have to start somewhere.

"What's so damned important, Joe?" Cliff asks as we sit down at a table inside the production tent, hot coffee mugs in hand. We're on a noon to midnight shooting day and I've dragged him away from the set at an inopportune time. Of course, for an a.d. any time is inopportune and his annoyance is showing. I'm exceedingly polite because I'd rather keep on his good side. He's trim and muscled, talks tough and backs it up, the kind of guy you'd want watching your back in a street fight and not the other way around.

"I'll give you the short answer, Cliff, and we'll go from there. Someone on your crew was involved in the murder of Carlotta Moreno."

"Bullshit," he says, disbelieving. "I know these guys."

"And a lot of them you haven't known for very long. Now just so you know, I'm working with the Sheriff on this. He's staying away officially because he thinks I have a better chance of getting information than he does." This last part is a lie. Time enough to bring Sergeant Ramos into the picture if and when I have something.

"You're serious."

"Damned right. So, how many of the crew did you work with before this picture, either as a first or a second, maybe even a third?"

He stares at me and I can see his mind working. Finally he says, "Maybe twenty five and I'd vouch for all of them."

"I'm going to need you to write their names down. Not now but some time before supper. Of your 25 or so, how many would you say are users?"

"You mean drugs?"

"That's what I mean."

"Is that why she was killed? Drugs?"

"We think so. So out of your 25—?"

"None. These are guys I asked for, guys I've worked with."

"That leaves us with 40 we don't know much about."

"Corky."

"What?"

"Corky Dupree," Coleman says. "The old guy. White hair."

"The gaffer," I say.

"That's right. Corky's a straight arrow and he's been around since the silents. If anybody can help you, Joe, it'll be Corky."

"Thanks."

"Catch him at dinner break. It'll be about five-thirty. I'll tell him you need to talk to him."

"Thanks, Cliff. One last thing. The 40 you don't know that well? Who's using?"

He hesitates. "I'm guessing but I figure four or five are into weed.

Nothing stronger. It hasn't hurt their work. I ignore it. "

"I'll need their names, too," I say. "All confidential. Your name won't come up."

"Right."

Coleman heads back to the set and I check my watch. A few minutes past three. I need to get back to the hotel in case Mick has called with an update on Sergeant Hector Ramos. I trudge back to my car, my cap pulled down low, hoping that Bob Aldrich doesn't spot me from afar. With Army back in the pokey, I have no time for rewrites.

I check at the desk. I have no messages so I presume Mick is still digging for dirt on Ramos and Bunny has yet to be told I won't be coming home this evening. I grab a container of coffee from the complimentary setup for guests in the lobby and head for my room. I sit down at the little writing desk where I dial police headquarters in downtown L.A. A minute later I have my friend Lt. Aaron Kleinschmidt on the phone.

"I'm on it," he says the moment we are connected.

"What do you mean, you're on it? You don't even know why I'm calling."

"Of course I do," Aaron says. "I talked to Mick Clausen early this morning. The poor guy is scared shitless, afraid you're going to be the victim of a gang hit. I told him I would take care of it which is why I have a squad car in East L.A. sitting on Tootie Reese. That is the reason you called, isn't it, Joe?"

"Well, not exactly," I mutter, lying through my teeth.

"No? Well, listen, my friend, those of us who love you, and that includes me and Mick, make it our life's work to protect you from yourself."

"Now wait a minute, Aaron—"

"A drug war involving Tootie Reese and the Mickey Cohen operation and you are in the middle of it? How in God's name do you manage to find your way into these predicaments?"

"It didn't start out that way, Aaron. At first it was just a missing person, then a murder—"

"Right. That old standby murder. Joe, if I had the manpower and it wasn't actually against the law, I'd send a couple of my guys down there to babysit you because that's what you need, a babysitter."

"Let me know when you're finished," I growl.

"Not even close, my friend. You are in possession of illegal narcotics, a major felony that carries with it a sentence of ten to twenty hard time in a federal facility—"

"I'm holding them until I can sort out who's who—"

"—not to mention the fact that all sorts of vindictive criminals would walk all over your dead body to get what you're holding."

"Aaron, you're making me feel very sorry I called you," I say.

"Well, don't be. My guys are all over Tootie like flypaper and I can dream up a dozen reasons to detain him should he decide to personally head in your direction."

"Thanks."

"However, if he sends a couple of his 'hood brothers, we might not catch that."

"Understood."

"Joe, you don't want my advice but I'm going to give it to you anyway. Get rid of the drugs. Hand them over to the sheriff or the local county prosecutor or Governor Brown for all I care but dump 'em—now!"

"Can't do it, Aaron. It's the only card I have to play."

"Then I'll be sure to send flowers."

There's a click as he disconnects. I stare at the phone. He's right. Of course he's right. I have no business hanging onto the drugs and no business being in the middle of this battle between Reese and Nedda Bloom and the Cohen organization. Bunny once said there's something of the Don Quixote in me, fighting unwinnable fights out of loyalty to a friend or sometimes just on principle. It's a failing I know I need to correct. It's just that I'm not sure how to do it.

I hear a sound behind me and whirl my head around. Rhonda is standing in the open connecting door between our two rooms. She's wearing a white terry cloth robe and a towel around her freshly washed hair.

"Sorry," she says sheepishly.

I ignore her apology. She's a drunk. She can't help drinking any more than a German Shepherd can help using a fire hydrant for a urInal.

"How are you feeling?" I ask.

"Okay, I guess. You don't need me around here any more, Joe, so I'm going back to Escondido to be with Pops."

"Bad idea. Your father can taken care of himself. You'd just be in the way."

"I'm in the way here," she says.

"Not so. Here you can be protected. Out on God's Little Acre, you'd be a clay pigeon. Or they might scoop you up to get to me. No, Rhonda, you stay at least for a day or two." I check my watch. It's pushing four-thirty. "Get dressed," I say, "and we'll drive out to the location. I'll introduce you to some movie stars."

Her eyes brighten.

"Elvis?"

I shake my head,

"Frankie Avalon? Ricky Nelson?"

"Let me surprise you," I say.

I drive into the parking area at the location around quarter past five. It's broad daylight and the company is still shooting. Luigi and Maria are setting up for the dinner break. I plop Rhonda down at one of the tables with a cup of coffee and tell her not to move as I start toward the plane wreck. As I pass the production tent, Rick Isaacs, the DGA trainee, pops out.

"Who's the babe, Mr. Bernardi?" he asks with a grin.

"What's the matter, Rick? Sherry dump you for somebody with a union card?"

He manages a wan smile. "Funny, old timer," he says and then heads for the dinner area with more than lasagna on his mind. Some guys live for the chase and Rick Isaacs seems to be one of them. Good luck with Rhonda, I think to myself. She just might have Rick for dessert.

As I draw close to the set, I hear Cliff Coleman shout "Dinner!" and the crew disbands. I head toward Corky Dupree who is talking to his Best Boy, chiding but not scolding, and apparently teaching the youngster a valuable lesson about the proper lighting of a set. The kid nods with a smile and hurries off as Corky turns his attention to me. He's a lean man, almost skinny, with longish white hair and a face that is at least fifty percent wrinkles, even more when he smiles which is often. He probably should have retired years ago but I've been told he's a widower with not much else in his life so he hangs on, setting the lights on movie after movie.

"Good evening, Mr. Bernardi," he says. "I'm told you want to chat."

"I do, Mr. Dupree."

"A favorite diversion of mine," he says, "and we'll do better if I'm Corky and you're Joe."

"As you wish, Corky. Why don't we grab trays and talk in the quiet of the tent? I'd rather we weren't overheard."

"So I understand."

A few minutes later we find ourselves staring at one another across trays of antipasto, pasta and a garlicky zuppa. With Miguel toes up at the local morgue, the hispanic side of the menu has dwindled to near zero. Gelato and tiramisu have been added.

"So, you want to know about our crew," Corky says.

"More precisely I want to know what you know about the crew.

I understand you once gaffed for Chaplin."

"I did, I did," he says. "More than once. Silent and sound. He was, ah, a perfectionist."

"You mean a tyrannical son of a bitch."

"Some would say that, those that did their jobs poorly. Mr. Chaplin and I never exchanged an unpleasant word."

"And over the years you've gotten to know a hell of a lot of crew members."

"Indeed and I know about others by reputation. Cliff tells me you suspect a bad apple is among us, a deadly bad apple with an appetite for narcotics."

"Not necessarily using but definitely selling."

Corky nods, popping a green olive in his mouth and then spitting out the pit.

"No one comes directly to mind. This is my first outing with the DGA trainee Isaacs, naturally. In a month or two he'll be working third assistant somewhere. Bright boy. Harry Jakes, the standby painter, is a total stranger. Likewise Bruno Koch in wardrobe. I hear he's a devious little fellow with roving hands. I wouldn't unzip my fly in front of him, he'd take it as an invitation. Rico Celli, the lens puller, says he's worked a lot overseas but he doesn't say much. Maybe it's a language barrier but he keeps to himself. And there's this fellow on the construction crew—Ziggy Kaplan. Usually these are local hires but Ziggy came down from L.A. with the company. And Joe, that's about it. The rest I know to a greater or lesser extent and I seriously doubt they are involved in anything even approaching narcotics or homicide."

I thank him for his help and we finish our meals while he regales me with stories about the good old days working with Frank Borzage and Lewis Milestone and George Sidney and another big name director who was caught en flagrante with a teenage starlet in his dressing room by Eleanor Roosevelt who often toured the studios during the war years. No doubt, Corky's seen it all.

Dinner over, it's back to work for Corky and I go in search of Rhonda who I find alone at one of the dinner tables putting away a glass of red wine. I pick up the glass and dump the contents on the ground.

"You've had enough of that stuff for the next ten weeks," I say. She glares up at me.

"I thought I was going to see movie stars," she whines.

"You did. You were sitting next to one."

"What? That fat ugly man? He's a movie star?"

I nod. "And he's got an Oscar to prove it."

"You're kidding me."

If I had the time and the inclination I would reveal to Rhonda the joys of 'Marty' but I have to get back to the hotel and feed Mick Clausen some names to check out. I grab Rhonda by the elbow and lead her to the car and without Elvis or some other teeny-bopper idol to warrant her attention she is only too happy to leave. I deposit her in her adjoining room and flip on her television set, then go into my room. The red light is blinking. Mick has called. I call him back.

"I could be wrong, Joe," Mick says, "but I think your guy Ramos is the real deal."

"Because?"

"Because of four years in the army, two of them as an infantry sergeant in Korea, two silver stars for bravery, first in his class at the police academy after he was mustered out. Letters of recommendation wherever he's served. You want more?"

"Then why did he not-so-subtly threaten me if I didn't turn the drugs over to him and I guarantee he didn't mean for safe keeping."

"Do you think maybe he might have been testing you, Joe? You're worried about his honesty. He might be just as worried about yours."

"Didn't occur to me," I say.

"Well, think about it. And while you're at it, think about this. Tootie Reese is a businessman but he's also homicidal and he'd slit your throat for the hell of it if he didn't need you any more. You might think the Cohen people are a little more civilized. They're not except in Nedda Isaacs' case, she'd have a bullet put in your brain by one of her people."

My brain suddenly engages.

"Whoa! What did you say?"

"I said Nedda wouldn't dirty her hands——"

"You said Nedda Isaacs."

"Yeah. Sorry. Force of habit. She was married to Moe Isaacs for seventeen years before she married that mope Jackie Bloom last year. I've always known her as Nedda Isaacs."

"She has a kid," I say.

"That's right. Two. The girl's going to school up north. Berkeley, I think. The son, Rick, he's a jerkoff. God knows what he's up to. My guess? Nothing good."

# CHAPTER EIGHTEEN

After a lengthy tutorial on the various gangland factions that rule the underbelly of Los Angeles, I hang up the phone and stare at the pieces of paper I have brought back with me from the set. One scrap has several names provided by Cliff Coleman, the other names from Corky Dupree, but it's obvious none of these names means a thing. None, save one. Rick Isaacs.

Rick Isaacs, a walking talking doofus, an amateur horndog with nothing on his mind but girls. His is a perfect cover, as slick as a newly waxed kitchen floor, and unless I am totally nuts, here is the young man who murdered Carlotta nee Linda and also dispatched Miguel Moreno to the hereafter. Young man? Seemingly nothing more dangerous than an overly hormonal teen but now the man behind the eyes has made himself visible. His pedigree speaks for itself. Father: Moe Isaacs, a sadistic enforcer with three known murders to his credit before he was gunned down last year outside a flower shop on Vermont Avenue. Mother: Nedda, a perfect compliment to her dead husband, vicious to the extreme, feared by her enemies as well as her closest associates. I can only imagine the terrifying threats that enabled Rick to get a foothold in the Guild. Worse yet, I can imagine what the Guild might be like a few years from now when Isaacs and his criminal cronies attempt to take control of the DGA in order to gain a stranglehold on the film industry.

I lean back in my chair and peer through the open door into the adjoining room. Rhonda is propped up on her bed, munching potato chips, and staring at a rerun of a network comedy that, despite the sound of raucous laughter, wasn't all that funny the first time around.

Fairly certain I won't be interrupted, I dial Sheriff's headquarters and after a few moments Ramos comes on the line.

"Ramos."

"We need to talk."

"Who is this?"

"You know who this is and you've got the wrong guy locked up."

"I've heard that song before, Bernardi. You're wasting my time."

"You've got the wrong guy, I've got the right guy."

I wait for him to hang up. He doesn't.

"Says who?" Ramos asks.

"Says me," I reply. "I'll be by the main entrance to Desert Sun Stadium at 7:30. I won't be hard to find."

"Of course not. There's nothing going on there. Come to the office."

"With what I have to say, you don't want to be seen with me. The stadium. 7:30. Come or not. Up to you."

I hang up and check my watch. Ten to seven. I decide to get there first and watch from the shadows, just to be safe. I cross over to the open doorway and tell Rhonda I'm going out. Lock both doors. Don't open for anyone but me. She nods as if she's heard me but I can't be sure. Gale Storm has her complete attention. I close the connecting door, lock it and head out.

The empty and little-used stadium is close by. It takes me six minutes to drive over and park in the shadows across the way. My watch reads 7:10. A minute later a squad car drives by slowly, disappears, then comes back and pulls up to the entrance. I'm not the only one making an early appearance. I watch as Ramos exits the vehicle and walks to the archway that leads into the stadium. He hesitates, assessing his surroundings. Confident that he is alone, I get out of the Galaxie and stride quickly across the street. Ramos sees me coming.

"Okay, Bernardi, I'm here. Talk fast and make sense or I'm gone."

"Let's step inside where we won't be observed," I say.

The sun is lowering itself into the Pacific, the stadium is being enveloped in shadow and Ramos and I face each other next to a shuttered refreshment stand.

"I'm waiting," Ramos says.

"You're nowhere on this case, Sergeant. You think you have Army McLeod for Miguel Moreno but you don't. My sense of honor won't let me leave until my friend is clear of any charges and if I wait for you to come up with the right answers, I might not get home until Christmas."

"Finished? Good. Don't bother to call me again, Bernardi."

He starts off.

"I've been told you're an honest cop, Sergeant, that beneath that badge beats the heart of a patriot who knows the difference between right and wrong, good and evil."

"Good night, Mr. Bernardi. Good night and goodbye," he says continuing toward the exit.

"Rick Isaacs!" I call after him.

He turns back to me.

"Who?"

"Rick Isaacs. He's working on the film as a trainee. His mother is Nedda Bloom, the de facto boss of Mickey Cohen's drug empire."

"And Isaacs killed Miguel Moreno?"

"That's right. And also Moreno's wife Carlotta."

"And you have proof of this?"

"Not yet," I say, "but I'll get it. I'll wear a wire."

He stares at me in disbelief.

"Are you out of your mind?"

"Not to the best of my knowledge. At least not yet."

"I don't get it, Bernardi. You'd actually go up against a narcotics kingpin wearing a wire? What's in this for you?"

"Not much, Sergeant, other than a debt to pay. Right now I am sick of my friend, sick of the lousy movie, sick of drugs and sick of you. I want to hop a plane and get back to my wife and kid. I also want to see my doctor lest I drop dead in the middle of this godforsaken cowtown. Well, Sarge, I get to go when Army McLeod is out of your jail and if that means poking a rattler with a sharp stick, that's what I'm going to do. My question is, are you in or out?"

After much back and forth Ramos declares himself 'in' but not before warning me that he will bear no responsibility if I get my head blown off. I assure him that, come Christmas, Santa will not hold it against him. Now comes the hard part, luring Isaacs out from behind his carefully constructed cover. I have the germ of a plan revolving in my head. All I need do is smooth the rough edges and lay out the bait where even a blind squirrel couldn't miss it.

Ramos heads back to headquarters, I drive back to the hotel where I place a long overdue phone call to my wife.

"Where are you?" Bunny asks.

"Yuma," I say.

"Let me rephrase my question. Why aren't you here, Joe?" There's very little warmth in her voice.

"Something came up. A last minute glitch. I need another day. Two at the most. Then I'll be home no matter what the situation here."

I endure a long silence. For a moment I think she's hung up. Then she says, "What's going on, Joe, and I don't mean in Yuma."

"What do you mean?"

"Two hours ago I got a call from Mt. Sinai hospital. You missed a scheduled treadmill test ordered for you by your so-called diet doctor. James P. McCaffrey, Allied Cardiology Partnership on Santa Monica Boulevard? Is that the guy, Joe? Your dietician?"

"Bunny, I'm fine," I say lamely.

"Fine? How can you be fine, Joe, when a cardiologist is ordering tests for you, tests your wife knows nothing about?"

"I didn't want to worry you."

"Well, you've done a piss poor job of that," she says irritably

"Listen to me. I mean it. I've been overly tired lately. Lev sent me to this guy as a precaution and he says it could be nothing."

"But it could be something."

"Sure, anything's possible but he didn't sound all that worried so neither am I."

"I want you home now, Joe."

"I can't. I owe Army, Bunny. Two days max, then I'm outta here. Promise."

Silence for a moment, then coldly and quietly she says, "Try not to die on us, Joe. I'm not sure Yvette could handle it." She hangs up. I stare at the phone and then I,too, hang up.

Annoyed, I walk over to the connecting door and open it. Rhonda's right where I left her but working on her third or fourth bag of chips. She smiles at me. From the TV set come the voices of Eddie Albert and Eva Gabor who have sold their dignity for big paychecks playing straight to a pig named Arnold. Eddie sneezes. The laugh machine laughs. I wonder how long it will be before the movies start sweetening their sound tracks; guffaws for Bob Hope, sobs for Joan Crawford.

"Don't sleep late tomorrow, Rhonda," I say to her. "I'm taking you home."

Her smile turns into a broad grin. She blows me a kiss, then turns her attention back to Eddie and Eva. I shut the door and then flop down on the bed. I stare up at the ceiling forcing my brain to turn my half-baked idea into a full fledged plan of action.

I'm up at seven and at headquarters by seven thirty where I explain my plan to Ramos. He buys into it even though there's risk involved. On that we agree. I briefly consider calling Angie to let her know what I'm up to but then dismiss it as a bad idea. On this point, Ramos and I also agree. There is nothing she can do to help and she can only get in the way. Better, too, that Army remain in the dark.

Ramos wires me up with a battery pack taped into the small of my back and masked by my loose fitting sports jacket. I'm carrying a pack of cigarettes in my breast pocket with a miniature mike nestled just below it. By reaching for a cigarette and pressing down hard on the pack, I can activate the recording device which can hold 30 minutes of conversation. We test the unit. It works perfectly. Next stop, the location.

Since the company filmed until midnight last night, the first shot won't be until ten o'clock at the earliest. I pull into the parking area by the motor homes at 9:15 and go looking for Cliff Coleman. He's not hard to find. I follow the sound of his voice into the production tent where he is chewing out the propmaster over some minor shortcoming. He cuts it short when he sees me and we huddle in the back of the tent. I tell him what I'm up to and what I need him for and he's in. A few minutes later he's gathered a bunch of us at a table, laying out the day's schedule. The second and third assistant directors are on hand along with Rick Isaacs, the Director of Photography Joe Biroc and the attractive young production assistant, Sherry Banks.

"As you know, Army McLeod is still in custody and normally, Joe would be pitching in. However Joe has to drive to Escondido on police business. He has to pick up something for Sergeant Ramos of the Sheriff's Department that bears on Army's case so he won't be back until at least four o'clock. Before then we're on our own as far as script changes go and if necessary we'll shoot around any problem."

Without being obvious, I glance sideways at Rick Isaacs hoping for a reaction. I get none. I make a note not to play poker with this guy. Cliff rambles on for a few more minutes but the trap has been baited. Now we wait to see what Isaacs is going to do about it. The meeting breaks up and I head out toward my car, stopping at the catering truck for a container of coffee. I look back toward the tent where Isaacs has Cliff by the arm and is deep into some sort of animated spiel. I doubt he's trying to sell him Tupperware. Then Isaacs hurries off toward his car and Cliff heads in my direction.

"The kid says he woke up this morning with a humungous toothache and needs to see a dentist right away," Cliff says, hitting up Luigi for a coffee of his own. "I told him to take the rest of the day off."

"Strike one," I say with a grin.

Cliff nods.

"You watch your ass out there, Joe," he says.

"I intend to," I tell him.

I swing by the Coronado and find Rhonda sitting on a sofa in the lobby with her overnight case beside her. She's dressed nicely enough but she looks like she's just gone three rounds with Sonny Liston.

"What happened? You run out of makeup?" I ask.

"Couldn't sleep last night. Charlie Chan kept me awake."

"Did you eat?"

"Coffee and a danish."

"Okay, then. Let's go."

Pretty soon we're on Rte. 80 heading west and I'm relating to Rhonda the plan to nail Rick Isaacs. It's the least I can do. A big part of it may take place at her little house on the outskirts of

Escondido. Several deputies with the San Diego County Sheriff's Department may already be posted inside alongside Rhonda's dad. Ramos will be in an unmarked car about a mile back, keeping his eye on me from afar and looking for signs of Rick Isaacs. At an average speed of sixty miles an hour, that puts Ramos about one minute behind me in the event something unexpected pops up. I plan to swing by Keefer's Storage and pick up the packages, then drive to Pop's hoping that somewhere along the way after I have the drugs, Isaacs will make his move. He may act right away or wait until I pull up to the house. I fully expect the latter. The house is isolated. County roads are not.

I try to work up some conversation with Rhonda but it's hopeless. Her head keeps lolling and her eyes keep closing and finally I pull over to the side of the road. I open her door and help her into the back seat where she can stretch out and not risk a broken neck. At first she tries to object but before I can even shut the rear door, she's snuggled into the fetal position and is already half-asleep. I get back behind the wheel and continue on, passing the little service station and then the Pine Valley turnoff. Forty minutes after that I exit onto Interstate 15 and head north toward Escondido.

Rhonda is still asleep on the back seat when I turn into the driveway of Keefer's Moving and Storage. I drive directly to the rear of the premises where the storage units are lined up on either side of the driveway and pull to a stop a few yards away from Unit 21. I get out of the car, walk over and punch in 4646 into the keypad of the remote. Immediately, the door unlocks and rolls up as the interior light goes on. I duck my head slightly and step inside. On the back wall is the shelf and on the shelf are the three packages I stored there days earlier. A feeling of relief starts to wash over me. Even if Isaacs doesn't take the bait, all I have to do is load up the car, take the drugs to Ramos and then drive to the airport to catch the next flight to Los Angeles. I will be done with a capital D and none too soon.

I'm about to grab one of the packages when I hear his voice.

"Don't make any sudden moves, Mr. Bernardi. I'm holding a gun and I will shoot you if I have to,. Please don't force my hand."

He's obviously standing in the open doorway and I don't have to see his face to know who it is.

# CHAPTER NINETEEN

Slowly I turn. Framed in the open doorway is Rick Isaacs. Funny, but with a .45 automatic clasped in his hand, he no longer looks like a clueless post-teen skirt chaser. Something in the eyes. They are cold and remorseless.

"Not very friendly, Rick."

"Deep down I'm not friendly at all, Mr. Bernardi. I have to hand it to you. I'd have sworn you were a grown up Boy Scout and here you are, down and dirty with the rest of us."

I reach up to my shirt pocket and press down hard on my cigarette pack, activating the wire recorder. I start to take the pack from my pocket but Isaacs stops me.

"Put it back. You won't live long enough to smoke it."

"Murder seems to be habit forming with you, Rick." I say with a devil-may-care smile, confident that Sergeant Ramos is right behind me and probably pulling up outside even as we speak.

"Only when scum like you get in my way. Who'd you make a deal with? Tootie Reese? Yeah, of course. Who else? Ramos is a straight arrow and the Sheriff is an egotistical jerk who's too busy banging some local school teacher to know what's going on."

I shrug.

"Buyers come in all shapes and sizes and they are not all in

California, Rick. I don't think your mother's going to be very proud of you, screwing up the way you have."

"I don't give a rat's ass what my mother thinks," Isaacs says."And nobody has screwed up anything as you can plainly see."

"Two murders, neither of them necessary? Your mother's too much a business woman to go down that road. A lot of cops will wink at drugs but they take murder seriously. What was it with Carlotta, Rick? Not only did she double cross you with Tootie Reese but she wouldn't put out? Not for a good looking stud like you? Shame on her. I'll bet she didn't know what she was missing."

"You see, Bernardi, that's where you're wrong. Her and me we were getting it on almost from the first day we showed up to make the picture. Mom told me to stay away from her so naturally I had to try a piece of the pie. I was merely cementing relations between business partners and she couldn't get enough of me."

"Doesn't sound like much of a motive for murder to me."

"Yeah. Well, something happened. Suddenly she started getting squirrelly on me. I figured it had something to do with that McLeod guy. About him I didn't care all that much—screwing is screwing and nothing special—but when she crossed me on our business arrangement, that was something else. First she said she didn't touch base with the guy across the border. He never showed. Then the next next day it was quality. The guy was trying to unload garbage merchandise at premium prices. Then a guy I know tells me she's made a deal on her own with Reese and I catch up with her just before she's going to run out on her husband leaving us both pulling our puds."

"You worked her over pretty good."

He nods.

"I did but she was a pretty tough babe and when I realized she wasn't going to turn over the goods, I put her out of her misery, figuring to get the stuff from Tootie Reese."

"And Miguel?"

"He figured I did his wife and he threatened me. Threatened me! The guy'd actually been in love with that two-timing bitch. Can you beat it? She doesn't give a crap about him but he can't see it. Love. What bullshit. Anyway he threatens me so I do him before he does me."

Right now I'm listening intently for any sign that Ramos is close by but I see or hear nothing. I get a queasy feeling that I'm on my own.

"Mama couldn't have approved of that, Rick," I say, stalling. "That wasn't business, that was personal."

He laughs.

"Like I care what Mama thinks. By the end of the year she's going to be out, both her and that pansy husband of hers, and I'm going to be splitting up L.A. with Tootie Reese. Unlike my mother I have no personal animosity toward Tootie, even if he did kill my old man. It was business, just business, even though people don't usually kill people over business."

"I'm glad to hear it," I say.

"There are exceptions," he says as he reaches in his pocket and takes out a silencer and carefully starts to screw it into the barrel of the automatic. "You're not one of us, Bernardi. You can't be relied upon. Sorry."

There are times like this when I wish I had my Beretta handy but carelessly I'd left it in the glove compartment of the car. I do, however, still have the keypad in my right hand and I'm pretty sure Isaacs hasn't noticed it. I press the button and pray.

The door lurches into action and starts to descend. Startled, Isaacs turns and looks back. In that instant I hurl myself at him, knocking his gun aside and sending us both to the floor. We grapple as the door continues down and then it settles and locks, the lights go out and the unit is plunged into total darkness. There is not a glimmer of light. It is as if I am in the bowels of a coal mine.

I cannot see past my eyelashes.

I feel a tightness in my chest as I kick Isaacs and scrabble away from him, curling up in the far corner of the unit. I hear him groan and I freeze in place, terrified to make a sound, terrified to breathe. Somewhere on the floor lies the gun but I dare not grope for it. The kid is in good shape and has me by twenty years. I cannot best him mano a mano, especially in my condition.

He's moving now, not close, not yet. Is he looking for me or for the gun? Does it matter? In a matter of minutes he will find me and I have no way to defend myself. I think of Bunny and Yvette and fight back my fear. His movements are coming closer. I can hear him breathing now as he probes the darkness. Closer. Much closer.

Suddenly a hand clamps onto my ankle. He makes a guttural sound as he leaps on top of me. He lashes out wildly, flailing his fists, catching me on the face and neck and shoulders. I try to fight him off. In the melee he grabs my right hand and as he does somehow the button on the key pad gets pushed. I hear a click and then the door starts to open. The lights go on and his face is inches from mine. It breaks into a maniacal grin and then he whips his head around, his gaze falling on the automatic pistol a few feet away. He dives for it, grabs it and staggers to his feet, pointing the weapon at me. I close my eyes and turn my head. The blast of the shot fills the tiny unit and my ears ring but I feel no pain. I freeze in place. Still no pain. I open my eyes and look. Isaacs is lying in a heap next to my feet, eyes sightless. Rhonda is standing in the open doorway, a .38 snub-nosed revolver in hand.

"Who was it said two guns are better than one? Was it me? I can't remember," she says with a grin.

"If you say so," I reply, struggling to get to my feet, which I do but not for long. Suddenly, I'm dizzy. The world around me spins out of control and I feel myself falling to the ground. Just before I pass out I think I hear the wail of police sirens. Ramos? What took him so long? Maybe he stopped for doughnuts.

I wish I could tell you what happened next. I can't. Not in detail. Images pop in and out of my brain. I am aware of being picked up and trundled onto a gurney. I am riding somewhere and I can hear those sirens again but now they are close by. Very close. Busting my eardrums. I'm being jounced around. Finally we stop. Rough hands grab me. Another gurney. I'm being wheeled somewhere. A white ceiling and white walls fly by. A loudspeaker keeps calling for a blue cold, whatever that is. People in scrubs keep leaning over me and staring me in the face. A fat little bald man tells me to start counting backwards from 100 and then he puts this mask over my face and I feel myself relaxing. Later, how much later I do not know, I think I smell fermaldehyde. Or is it embalming fluid? Where am I? Am I dead? I smell flowers but I don't hear an organ playing 'Nearer my God to Thee'. I take that as a good sign. Then I see Bunny. She's talking to a man in a white coat. He nods. She nods. I think I spy red roses and white carnations and then I slip back into darkness again.

"Joe? Joe, are you awake?"

It's Bunny's voice. I force my eyes open. She's hovering over me, looking at me anxiously.

"Joe," she whispers quietly and leans down and presses her face against mine and I can hear tiny sobs and her cheek is getting moist.

"Hi, kid. Is it you?" I manage to ask.

"It's me, Joe. It's me," she says, kissing my face.

"Where am I?"

"Mercy Hospital in San Diego."

"Not dead?"

"Not yet, tough guy," she says.

I reach out my arms and pull her close to me. I savor the warmth of her body and the softness of her. We could have stayed that way forever but an alert nurse caught what was going on and showed up to give me a going over: temperature and blood pressure for sure, other pricks and probes I was not that keen about. That guy in the white coat shows up and tells me what a great job he did saving my life. Another 48 hours and I'd have been checking into Forest Lawn. I am now sporting two arterial stents which have given new life to my heart. There's nothing I won't be able to do, he says. Great, I tell him. Will I be able to play the accordion, I ask. He doesn't see why not, he says. Terrific, I tell him. I never could before. He smiles out of politeness but obviously has no sense of humor. Doesn't he know the old jokes are the best?

Yvette and Bridget make an appearance. My daughter wants to know why I am goofing off in bed and am I sick and if I am, what's the matter with me? I tell her the doctors have fixed me up with a better heart which was breaking down because I missed her so. She gives me an 'Oh yeah' look. There are some things even a ten year old won't fall for.

That evening Sergeant Ramos shows up with Angie Garcia. They've brought a grateful Army with them. Bunny and Angie smile in friendly greeting. When Angie isn't looking, Bunny gives her a dirty look. Rhonda fares just about as well. It is nice to know that I am so highly prized by my loving wife. I'll remind her of the fact the next time she tells me what a doofus I am.

All is well in Yuma. Rick Isaacs is dead and the wire recording exonerates Army. Ramos has made a copy and send it off to Nedda Bloom, drawing her attention to her son's anticipated palace coup that would have reduced Nedda to a nonentity in the Cohen organization. To do otherwise risked turning the little weasel into a martyred son not worth one of Nedda's salty tears. The drugs have been catalogued and secured but they won't be around long. Unneeded for a trial that will never take place, next week the contraband will be incinerated. Tootie Reese will be heartbroken but not for long. Mexico is a big country and Tootie knows a lot of people.

# CHAPTER TWENTY

Two weeks have passed. I am at home with Bunny and Yvette and as happy as it's possible to be when treated like a man who may be on the verge of attending his own funeral. The first three days were spent in bed where I was waited on like the grand poobah of the Ottoman Empire. Bridget brought me my breakfast of Cream of Wheat, weak tea, and dry whole wheat toast. Lunch consisted of a glop of yogurt, weak tea and whole wheat toast smothered with a dollop of margarine. Dinner was far more varied. I've had boiled chicken, roasted chicken and sauteed chicken. These dishes were festooned with boiled tomatoes, celery stalks and raw carrots. Dessert was sugar free, fat free rhubarb pudding which had had all the flavor boiled out of it. The third night I asked Bridget to hold the pudding and bring me the flavor. She laughed and brought me more pudding.

Lev Rosen showed up twice on forty dollar house calls. He listened to my heart and my chest, told me a dirty joke and invited me to his club to play golf which he knows full well I do not play. Jim McCaffrey, my cardiologist, also showed up twice, billing me eighty dollars a pop for his appearances. He, too, listened to my heart, seemed satisfied, and related the story of a favorite patient of his, 33 years old, who dropped dead in his driveway as he was about to get into his car. Hospital personnel found traces of Cream of Wheat on his shirt when they examined him. Jim didn't bother inviting me for golf.

On the fourth day I was permitted to get out of bed, wander about in my bathrobe and watch a little television. By the end of that fourth day, that's what I was watching. A little television. Actually, very little television. Newton Minow, the one time FCC chairman, had it right. Television, at least during daylight hours, is a vast wasteland. I am itching to get back to my book but McCaffrey has nixed the idea for at least a week. He doesn't want me getting roiled up emotionally as I tend to do when adventuring along with my fictitious characters. He prescribed daytime TV and now I understand why. In a bottle it would outsell sleeping pills.

On the fifth day, Army McLeod drops in to pay his respects. The Phoenix has wrapped principal photography and he is no longer needed. He thanks me for the umpteenth time for saving his ass. I reply it was a delight to make things right for an old and dear friend. I invite him for supper but when he hears the menu, he demurs. Tofu in wine sauce accompanied by swiss chard and lentil beans has about as much appeal as a porno movie starring Victor Buono and Hope Emerson.

Day Six arrives and I am allowed into my office and permitted to look at my typewriter. Not use it, just look at it. I may if I wish write long overdue letters to old friends. I may touch base with other dear friends by phone. Bertha and Glenda Mae are at the top of my list. Aaron, Ray and Mick are verboten as they were involved in my heart pounding adventure with narcotics. Reliving those days could be hazardous to my health, so says Jim McCaffrey. I am being protected and pampered and living in a cocoon and I can't stand it.

Comes the seventh day and I am liberated. I am allowed to rescue Sam August from Gunderson's two thugs. The trouble is, I've been away from my story for so long I've forgotten the clever way

I was going to do it. I sit staring at a blank sheet of paper. I am in agony. I know I had something worked out, chilling and original and even funny. One of Sam's finest moments and now I can't remember what it was.

I get a beep-beep from my intercom and Bridget intrudes on my musing.

"You have company, sir. The fat fellow in funny clothes who never cuts his hair. Shall I send him up?"

This is a rare treat. A home visit from Phineas.

"Please do, Bridget," I say.

"And will he be staying for lunch, sir?"

"Not when he sees what you have on the menu."

"And a very good morning to you as well, sir," she says brittlely, followed by something unintelligible muttered under her breath.

I hear him galumphing up the stairs and a few moments later he appears in my open doorway, wheezing from exertion.

"You know, Phineas, you could afford to lose a few extra pounds," I say to him.

"Exactly what my former doctor said to me only last month. My new doctor thinks I am the picture of health and carry my weight admirably on my substantial frame."

"Wait a second. Your doctor tries to put you on a diet so the next day you go out and find a doctor who will validate your skewed vision of yourself."

"Wrong, old top. It was not the next day, it was the second day after two other quacks proved to be unacceptable. He has put me on a regimen that includes some of my favorite sauces and desserts. There is, for example, great nutritional value in Hollandaise sauce, but of course you already knew that." With that Phineas plops down on my office sofa, exhaling loudly as he does so.

"Well, I think you're being very shortsighted about your physical condition, my friend, but before you leave, I want you to give

192

me the name and phone number. of this new doctor of yours. Just a precaution in case Lev Rosen decides to retire."

"Done," he says. "So have you heard from the Mirisches?"

"Why should I hear from the Mirisches?"

"Because there is a rumor afloat that they have just made an offer for the movie rights to Sam August."

"First I've heard of it."

"I've also been told that they have offered a lucrative three-picture deal to an obscure young actor named Robert Redford. He's in the new Natalie Wood movie—"

"I know who he is," I say.

"Methinks there is a connection."

"As I said, I know nothing about it."

"But he would make a smashing Sam August, don't you think?"

"Possibly."

"Nothing from Barry?"

"A get well card."

"But he is still your agent? You haven't scared him off."

"I haven't fired him, if that's what you mean."

"Yes. Well, then I will track him down."

He gets to his feet.

"By the way," he says, "did you hear about Simon Starbuck?"

"What about him?"

"Dead as a carp, face down in a plate of linguini at the NBC commissary."

"You're joking."

"Upon my honor, old top. Heart attack. Dead before his face hit the alfredo sauce."

"My God."

"He was dining with three programming executives who were raking him over the coals for going a hundred thousand over budget on every episode of 'Galaxy Trek' and not properly handling Hank

Baxter, his knuckle-headed star, Broadway's gift to the theater with one Tony and fourteen flops to his credit. They wouldn't let Simon fire the guy and they wouldn't back him up whenever there was a dispute. A few days ago Baxter was demanding to be made a producer with script and director approval. Granted, you needn't be a brain surgeon to produce television, not even a decent veterinarian, but an actor? Talk about the lunatics running the asylum. Anyway, the man who gave heart attacks, not got them, was hoist on his own petard. A memorial service is scheduled for Friday evening and those who loved and respected him will no doubt be in attendance. I understand the family has booked a very small venue."

"Sad in a way," I say.

"Not really," Phineas says. "Even Caesar had it coming and Starbuck was no Caesar. Well, toodle-oo, old top. I am off in quest of material for tomorrow's column. Love to dear Bunny."

With a smile and a wave he leaves. I am torn. I didn't like Simon Starbuck but no man deserves to die at such an early age, even though he willingly took part in the blood sport called television programming. On the other hand I am intrigued by what Phineas told me about a possible movie deal.

Just then the phone rings. I pick up. Improbably it is my agent Barry Loeb about whom we were just talking. He has wonderful news. I listen carefully, trying to act surprised. The Mirisch Brothers. Excellent. Who? Robert Redford. Know his work well from television. A terrific idea. Would it be okay if he dropped by at dinnertime? Of course. I invite him to eat with us but only if he is partial to steamed cabbage, boiled potatoes, and baked eggplant. There is a long silence and then we settle for Scandia's tomorrow for lunch.

THE END

# AUTHOR'S NOTE

Like the eighteen books that preceded it in this series, 'Ashes to Ashes" is a work of fiction peppered with imaginative participation by real life people whose actions and dialogue have been totally invented by the author. As a motion picture 'The Flight of the Phoenix' was quite real. So, too, were Mickey Cohen and the criminal Tootie Reese but the events regarding drug dealing and murder did not happen. At least not to my knowledge and as for the Sheriff of Yuma County in 1965, I'm sure he was nothing like Joshua Dixon. When released the reaction to 'The Flight of the Phoenix' was mixed though generally favorable. In the years since then it has taken on cult status. Mostly the critics carped about the unlikely ability of the crew and passengers to rebuild a wrecked airplane into a credible flying machine with only crude hand tools available in the middle of the desert but the film was lauded for its adventuresome nature, the quality of story telling and the excellent performances by an all-male cast. It received two Oscar nominations, one for actor Ian Bannen and another for film editor Michael Luciano. At the box office it failed to recoup its budget of $5.3 million taking in slightly more than $3.0 million. Still, like 'Citizen Kane' contemporary dismissal when it was released could not dim the growing respect it enjoyed in the years that followed. And then in 2004 Twentieth Century Fox released a remake with an inferior cast and a poorly constructed script that generally ignored the original novel by Elleston Trevor. Grossing $34.5 million on a budget of $45 million it was a critical and financial failure with devastating negative reviews. *The New York Times* called it a "rickety update of the far superior 1965 movie" and this version has not grown in reputation in subsequent years. Maybe I'm just a cranky old movie buff but why do these newbies fresh from film school insist on remaking movies that were done right the first time. Do we all remember with affection the original Frank Sinatra version of 'The Manchurian Candidate', an artistic triumph with a magnificent Oscar-worthy performance by Angela Lansbury as Raymond Shaw's cold and calculating mother? Does anyone remember the dreadful and confusing mishmosh of a remake with Denzel Washington? The incomparable Meryl Streep tried to top Ms. Lansbury's performance. She failed. Note to Hollywood. Remake the ones you screwed up the first time around. That, at least, makes a modicum of sense. On a somber note, tragedy struck during the original filming when stunt pilot Paul Manz was killed doing a flyby in the rebuilt 'Phoenix'. The picture is dedicated to his memory.

# ABOUT THE AUTHOR

**Peter S. Fischer** is a former television writer-producer who currently lives in the Monterey Bay area of Central California. He is a co-creator of "Murder, She Wrote" for which he wrote over 40 scripts. Among his other credits are a dozen "Columbo" episodes and a season helming "Ellery  Queen." He has also written and produced several TV mini-series and Movies of the Week. In 1985 he was awarded an Edgar by the Mystery Writers of America. In addition to four EMMY nominations, two Golden Globe Awards for Best TV series, and an Anthony Award from the Boucheron, he has received the IBPA award for the Best Mystery Novel of the Year, a Bronze Medal from the Independent Publishers Association and an Honorable Mention from the San Francisco Festival for his first novel.

Available at Amazon.com

www.petersfischer.com

# PRAISE FOR THE HOLLYWOOD MURDER MYSTERIES

## Jezebel in Blue Satin

*In this stylish homage to the detective novels of Hollywood's Golden Age, a press agent stumbles across a starlet's dead body and into the seamy world of scheming players and morally bankrupt movie moguls.....An enjoyable fast-paced whodunit from opening act to final curtain.*

—Kirkus Reviews

*Fans of golden era Hollywood, snappy patter and Raymond Chandler will find much to like in Peter Fischer's murder mystery series, all centered on old school studio flak, Joe Bernardi, a happy-go-lucky war veteran who finds himself immersed in tough situations.....The series fills a niche that's been superseded by explosions and violence in too much of popular culture and even though jt's a world where men are men and women are dames, its glimpses at an era where the facade of glamour and sophistication hid an uglier truth are still fun to revisit.*

—2012 San Francisco Book Festival, Honorable Mention

*Jezebel in Blue Satin, set in 1947, finds movie studio publicist Joe Bernardi slumming it at a third rate motion picture house running on large egos and little talent. When the ingenue from the film referenced in the title winds up dead, can Joe uncover the killer before he loses his own life? Fischer makes an effortless transition from TV mystery to page turner, breathing new life into the film noir hard boiled detective tropes. Although not a professional sleuth, Joe's evolution from everyman into amateur private eye makes sense; any bad publicity can cost him his job so he has to get to the bottom of things.*

—ForeWord Review

## We Don't Need No Stinking Badges

*A thrilling mystery packed with Hollywood glamour, intrigue and murder, set in 1948 Mexico.....Although the story features many famous faces (Humphrey Bogart, director John Huston, actor Walter Huston and novelist B. Traven, to name a few), the plot smartly focuses on those behind the scenes. The big names aren't used as gimmicks—they're merely planets for the story to rotate around. Joe Bernardi is the star of the show and this fictional tale in a real life setting (the actual set of 'Treasure of the Sierra Madre' was also fraught with problems) works well in Fischer's sure hands....A smart clever Mexican mystery.*

### —Kirkus Reviews

*A former TV writer continues his old-time Hollywood mystery series, seamlessly interweaving fact and fiction in this drama that goes beyond the genre's cliches. "We Don't Need No Stinking Badges" again transports readers to post WWII Tinseltown inhabited by cinema publicist Joe Bernardi... Strong characterization propels this book. Toward the end the crosses and double-crosses become confusing, as seemingly inconsequential things such as a dead woman who was only mentioned in passing in the beginning now become matters on which the whole plot turns (but) such minor hiccups should not deter mystery lovers, Hollywood buffs or anyone who adores a good yarn.*

### —ForeWord Review

*Peter S. Fischer has done it again—he has put me in a time machine and landed me in 1948. He has written a fast paced murder mystery that will have you up into the wee hours reading. If you love old movies, then this is the book for you.*

### —My Shelf. Com

*This is a complex, well-crafted whodunit all on its own. There's plenty of action and adventure woven around the mystery and the characters are fully fashioned. The addition of the period piece of the 1940's filmmaking and the inclusion of big name stars as supporting characters is the whipped cream and cherry on top. It all comes together to make an engaging and fun read.*

### —Nyssa, Amazon Customer Review

## Love Has Nothing to Do With It

*Fischer's experience shows in 'Love Has Nothing To Do With It', an homage to film noir and the hard-boiled detective novel. The story is complicated... but Fischer never loses the thread. The story is intricate enough to be intriguing but not baffling....Joe Bernardi's swagger is authentic and entertaining. Overall he is a likable sleuth with the dogged determination to uncover the truth.... While the outcome of the murder is an unknown until the final pages of the current title, we do know that Joe Bernardi will survive at least until 1950, when further adventures await him in the forthcoming 'Everybody Wants an Oscar'.*

    —Clarion Review

*A stylized, suspenseful Hollywood whodunit set in 1949....Goes down smooth for murder-mystery fans and Old Hollywood junkies.*

    —Kirkus Review

*The Hollywood Murder Mysteries just might make a great Hallmark series. Let's give this book: The envelope please: FIVE GOLDEN OSCARS.*

    —Samfreene, Amazon Customer Review

*The writing is fantastic and, for me, the topic was a true escape into our past entertainment world. Expect it to be quite different from today's! But that's why readers will enjoy visiting Hollywood as it was in the past. A marvelous concept that hopefully will continue up into the 60s and beyond. Loved it!*

    —GABixlerReviews

## The Unkindness of Strangers

*Winner of the Benjamin Franklin Award
for Best Mystery Book of 2012
by the Independent Book Publisher's Association.*

## Book One—1947
## JEZEBEL IN BLUE SATIN

WWII is over and Joe Bernardi has just returned home after three years as a war correspondent in Europe. Married in the heat of passion three weeks before he shipped out, he has come home to find his wife Lydia a complete stranger. It's not long before Lydia is off to Reno for a quickie divorce which Joe won't accept. Meanwhile he's been hired as a publicist by third rate movie studio, Continental Pictures. One night he enters a darkened sound stage only to discover the dead body of ambitious, would-be actress Maggie Baumann. When the police investigate, they immediately zero in on Joe as the perp. Short on evidence they attempt to frame him and almost succeed. Who really killed Maggie? Was it the over-the-hill actress trying for a comeback? Or the talentless director with delusions of grandeur? Or maybe it was the hapless leading man whose career is headed nowhere now that the "real stars" are coming back from the war. There is no shortage of suspects as the story speeds along to its exciting and unexpected conclusion.

## Book Two—1948
## WE DON'T NEED NO STINKING BADGES

Joe Bernardi is the new guy in Warner Brothers' Press Department so it's no surprise when Joe is given the unenviable task of flying to Tampico, Mexico, to bail Humphrey Bogart out of jail without the world learning about it. When he arrives he discovers that Bogie isn't the problem. So-called accidents are occurring daily on

Available in paperback or Kindle editions from Amazon.com

the set, slowing down the filming of "The Treasure of the Sierra Madre" and putting tempers on edge. Everyone knows who's behind the sabotage. It's the local Jefe who has a finger in every illegal pie. But suddenly the intrigue widens and the murder of one of the actors throws the company into turmoil. Day by day, Joe finds himself drawn into a dangerous web of deceit, dupliciity and blackmail that nearly costs him his life.

## Book Three—1949
## LOVE HAS NOTHING TO DO WITH IT

Joe Bernardi's ex-wife Lydia is in big, big trouble. On a Sunday evening around midnight she is seen running from the plush offices of her one- time lover, Tyler Banks. She disappears into the night leaving Banks behind, dead on the carpet with a bullet in his head. Convinced that she is innocent, Joe enlists the help of his pal, lawyer Ray Giordano, and bail bondsman Mick Clausen, to prove Lydia's innocence, even as his assignment to publicize Jimmy Cagney's comeback movie for Warner's threatens to take up all of his time. Who really pulled the trigger that night? Was it the millionaire whose influence reached into City Hall? Or the not so grieving widow finally freed from a loveless marriage. Maybe it was the partner who wanted the business all to himself as well as the new widow. And what about the mysterious envelope, the one that disappeared and everyone claims never existed? Is it the key to the killer's identity and what is the secret that has been kept hidden for the past forty years?

## Book Four—1950
## EVERYBODY WANTS AN OSCAR

After six long years Joe Bernardi's novel is at last finished and has been shipped to a publisher. But even as he awaits news, fingers crossed for luck, things are heating up at the studio. Soon production will begin on Tennessee Williams' "The Glass Menagerie" and Jane Wyman has her sights set on a second consecutive Academy Award. Jack Warner has just signed Gertrude Lawrence for the pivotal role of Amanda and is positive that the Oscar will go to Gertie. And meanwhile Eleanor Parker, who has gotten rave reviews for a prison picture called "Caged" is sure that 1950 is her year to take home the trophy. Faced with three very talented ladies all vying for his best efforts, Joe is resigned to performing a monumental juggling act. Thank God he has nothing else to worry about or at least that was the case until his agent informed him that a screenplay is floating around Hollywood that is a dead ringer for his newly completed novel. Will the ladies be forced to take a back seat as Joe goes after the thief that has stolen his work, his good name and six years of his life?

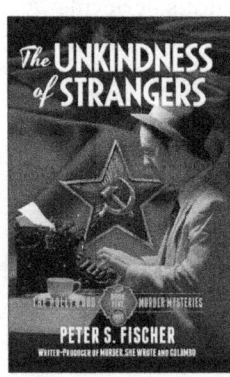

## Book Five—1951
## THE UNKINDNESS OF STRANGERS

Warner Brothers is getting it from all sides and Joe Bernardi seems to be everybody's favorite target. "A Streetcar Named Desire" is unproducible, they say. Too violent, too seedy, too sexy, too controversial and what's worse, it's being directed by that well-known pinko, Elia Kazan. To make matters worse, the country's number one hate monger, newspaper columnist Bryce Tremayne, is coming after Kazan with a vengeance and nothing Joe can do or say will stop him. A vicious expose column is set to run in every Hearst paper in the nation on the upcoming Sunday but a funny thing happens Friday night. Tremayne is found in a compromising condition behind the wheel of his car, a bullet hole between his eyes. Come Sunday and the scurrilous attack on Kazan does not appear. Rumors fly. Kazan is suspected but he's not the only one with a motive. Consider:

Elvira Tremayne, the unloved widow. Did Tremayne slug her one time too many?

Hubbell Cox, the flunky whose homosexuality made him a target of derision.

Willie Babbitt, the muscle. He does what he's told and what he's told to do is often unpleasant.

Jenny Coughlin, Tremayne's private secretary. But how private and what was her secret agenda?

Jed Tompkins, Elvira's father, a rich Texas cattle baron who had only contempt for his son-in-law.

Boyd Larabee, the bookkeeper, hired by Tompkins to win Cox's confidence and report back anything he's learned.

Annie Petrakis, studio makeup artist. Tremayne destroyed her lover. Has she returned the favor?

## Book Six–1952
## NICE GUYS FINISH DEAD

Ned Sharkey is a fugitive from mob revenge. For six years he's been successfully hiding out in the Los Angeles area while a $100, 000 contract for his demise hangs over his head. But when Warner Brothers begins filming "The Winning Team", the story of Grover Cleveland Alexander, Ned can't resist showing up at the ballpark to reunite with his old pals from the Chicago Cubs of the early 40's who have cameo roles in the film. Big mistake. When Joe Bernardi, Warner Brothers publicity guy, inadvertently sends a press release and a photo of Ned to the Chicago papers, mysterious people from the Windy City suddenly appear and a day later at break of dawn, Ned's body is found sprawled atop the pitcher's mound. It appears that someone is a hundred thousand dollars richer. Or maybe not. Who is the 22 year old kid posing as a 50 year old former hockey star? And what about Gordo Gagliano, a mountain of a man, who is out to find Ned no matter who he has to hurt to succeed? And why did baggy pants comic Fats McCoy jump Ned and try to kill him in the pool parlor? It sure wasn't about money. Joe , riddled with guilt because the photo he sent to the newspapers may have led to Ned's death, finds himself embroiled in a dangerous game of who-dun-it that leads from L. A. 's Wrigley Field to an upscale sports bar in Altadena to the posh mansions of Pasadena and finally to the swank clubhouse of Santa Anita racetrack.

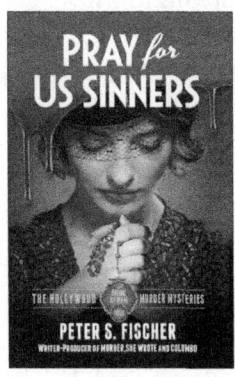

## Book Seven—1953
## PRAY FOR US SINNERS

Joe finds himself in Quebec but it's no vacation. Alfred Hitchcock is shooting a suspenseful thriller called "I Confess" and Montgomery Clift is playing a priest accused of murder. A marriage made in heaven? Hardly. They have been at loggerheads since Day One and to make matters worse their feud is spilling out into the newspapers. When vivacious Jeanne d'Arcy, the director of the Quebec Film Commisssion volunteers to help calm the troubled waters, Joe thinks his troubles are over but that was before Jeanne got into a violent spat with a former lover and suddenly found herself under arrest on a charge of first degree murder. Guilty or not guilty? Half the clues say she did it, the other half say she is being brilliantly framed. But by who? Fingers point to the crooked Gonsalvo brothers who have ties to the Buffalo mafia family and when Joe gets too close to the truth, someone tries to shut him up. . . permanently. With the Archbishop threatening to shut down the production in the wake of the scandal, Joe finds himself torn between two loyalties.

## Book Eight—1954
## HAS ANYBODY HERE SEEN WYCKHAM?

Everything was going smoothly on the set of "The High and the Mighty" until the cast and crew returned from lunch. With one exception. Wiley Wyckham, the bit player sitting in seat 24A on the airliner mockup, is among the missing, and without Wyckham sitting in place, director William Wellman cannot continue filming. A studio wide search is instituted. No Wyckham. A lookalike is hired that night, filming resumes the next day and still no Wyckham. Except that by this time, it's been discovered that Wyckham, a British actor, isn't really Wyckham at all but an imposter who may very well be an agent for the Russian government, The local police call in the FBI. The FBI calls in British counterintelligence. A manhunt for the missing actor ensues and Joe Bernardi, the picture's publicist, is right in the middle of the intrigue. Everyone's upset, especially John Wayne who is furious to learn that a possible Commie spy has been working in a picture he's producing and starring in. And then they find him . It's the dead of night on the Warner Brothers backlot and Wyckham is discovered hanging by his feet from a streetlamp, his body bloodied and tortured and very much dead. and pinned to his shirt is a piece of paper with the inscription "Sic Semper Proditor". (Thus to all traitors). Who was this man who had been posing as an obscure British actor? How did he smuggle himself into the country and what has he been up to? Has he been blackmailing an important higher-up in the film business and did the victim suddenly turn on him? Is the MI6 agent from London really who he says he is and what about the reporter from the London Daily Mail who seems to know all the right questions to ask as well all the right answers.

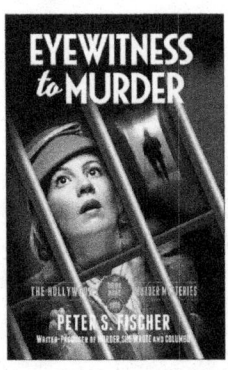

## Book Nine—1955
## EYEWITNESS TO MURDER

Go to New York? Not on your life. It's a lousy idea for a movie. A two year old black and white television drama? It hasn't got a prayer. This is the age of CinemaScope and VistaVision and stereophonic sound and yes, even 3-D. Burt Lancaster and Harold Hecht must be out of their minds to think they can make a hit movie out of "Marty". But then Joe Bernardi gets word that the love of his life, Bunny Lesher, is in New York and in trouble and so Joe changes his mind. He flies east to talk with the movie company and also to find Bunny and dig her out of whatever jam she's in. He finds that "Marty" is doing just fine but Bunny's jam is a lot bigger than he bargained for. She's being held by the police as an eyewitness to a brutal murder of a close friend in a lower Manhattan police station. Only a jammed pistol saved Bunny from being the killer's second victim and now she's in mortal danger because she knows what the man looks like and he's dead set on shutting her up. Permanently. Crooked lawyers, sleazy con artists and scheming businessmen cross Joe's path, determined to keep him from the truth and when the trail leads to the sports car racing circuit at Lime Rock in Connecticut, it's Joe who becomes the killer's prime target.

# Book Ten—1956
# A DEADLY SHOOT IN TEXAS

Joe Bernardi's in Marfa, Texas, and he's not happy. The tarantulas are big enough to carry off the cattle , the wind's strong enough to blow Marfa into New Mexico, and the temperature would make the Congo seem chilly. A few miles out of town Warner Brothers is shooting Edna Ferber's "Giant" with a cast that includes Rock Hudson, Elizabeth Taylor and James Dean and Jack Warner is paying through the nose for Joe's expertise as a publicist. After two days in Marfa Joe finds himself in a lonely cantina around midnight, tossing back a few cold ones, and being seduced by a gorgeous student young enough to be his daughter. The flirtation goes nowhere but the next morning little Miss Coed is found dead . And there's a problem. The coroner says she died between eight and nine o'clock. Not so fast, says Joe, who saw her alive as late as one a.m. When he points this out to the County Sheriff, all hell breaks loose and Joe becomes the target of some pretty ornery people. Like the Coroner and the Sheriff as well as the most powerful rancher in the county, his arrogant no-good son and his two flunkies, a crooked lawyer and a grieving father looking for justice or revenge, either one will do. Will Joe expose the murderer before the murderer turns Joe into Texas road kill? Tune in.

## Book Eleven–1957
## EVERYBODY LET'S ROCK

Big trouble is threatening the career of one of the country's hottest new teen idols and Joe Bernardi has been tapped to get to the bottom of it. Call it blackmail or call it extortion, a young woman claims that a nineteen year old Elvis Presley impregnated her and then helped arrange an abortion. There's a letter and a photo to back up her claim. Nonsense, says Colonel Tom Parker, Elvis's manager and mentor. It's a damned lie. Joe is not so sure but Parker is adamant. The accusation is a totally bogus and somebody's got to prove it. But no police can be involved and no lawyers. Just a whiff of scandal and the young man's future will be destroyed, even though he's in the midst of filming a movie that could turn him into a bona fide film star. Joe heads off to Memphis under the guise of promoting Elvis's new film and finds himself mired in a web of deceit and danger. Trusted by no one he searches in vain for the woman behind the letter, crossing paths with Sam Philips of Sun Records, a vindictive alcoholic newspaper reporter, a disgraced doctor with a seedy past, and a desperate con artist determined to keep Joe from learning the truth.

## Book Twelve—1958
## A TOUCH OF HOMICIDE

It takes a lot to impress Joe Bernardi. He likes his job and the people he deals with but nobody is really special. Nobody, that is, except for Orson Welles, and when Avery Sterling, a bottom feeding excuse for a producer, asks Joe's help in saving Welles from an industry-wide smear campaign, Joe jumps in, heedless that the pool he has just plunged into is as dry as a vermouthless martini. A couple of days later, Sterling is found dead in his office and the police immediately zero in on two suspects—Joe who has an alibi and Welles who does not. Not to worry, there are plenty of clues at the crime scene including a blood stained monogrammed handkerchief, a rejected screenplay, a pair of black-rimmed reading glasses, a distinctive gold earring and petals from a white carnation. What's more, no less than four people threatened to kill him in front of witnesses. A case so simple a two-year old could solve it but the cop on the case is a dimwit whose uncle is on the staff of the police commissioner. Will Joe and Orson solve the case before one of them gets arrested for murder? Will an out-of-town hitman kill one or both of them? Worst of all, will Orson leave town leaving Joe holding the proverbial bag?

## Book Thirteen—1959
## SOME LIKE 'EM DEAD

After thirteen years, the great chase is over and Joe Bernardi is marrying Bunny Lesher. After a brief weekend honeymoon, it'll be back to work for them both; Bunny at the Valley News where she has just been named Assistant Editor and Joe publicizing Billy Wilder's new movie, Some Like It Hot about two musicians hiding out from the mob in an all-girl band. It boasts a great script and a stellar cast that includes Tony Curtis, Jack Lemmon and Marilyn Monroe, so what could go wrong? Plenty and it starts with Shirley Davenport, Bunny's protege at the News, who has been assigned to the entertainment pages. To placate Bunny and against his better judgement Joe gives Shirley a press credential for the shoot and from the start, she is a destructive force, alienating cast and crew, including Billy Wilder, who does not suffer fools easily. Someone must have become really fed up with her because one misty morning a few hundred yards down the beach from the famed Hotel Del Coronado, Shirley's lifeless body, her head bashed in with a blunt instrument, is discovered by joggers. This after she'd been seen lunching with George Raft; hobnobbing with up and coming actor, Vic Steele; angrily ignoring fellow journalist Hank Kendall; exchanging jealous looks with hair stylist Evie MacPherson; and making a general nuisance of herself everywhere she turned. United Artists is aghast and so is Joe This murder has to be solved and removed from the front pages of America's newspapers as soon as possible or when it's released, this picture will be known as 'the murder movie', hardly a selling point for a rollicking comedy.

## Book Fourteen—1960
## DEAD MEN PAY NO DEBTS

Among the hard and fast rules in Joe Bernardi's life is this one:
Do not, under any circumstances, travel east during the winter months. In this way one avoids dealing with snow, ice, sleet, frostbite and pneumonia. Unfortunately he has had to break this rule and having done so, is paying the price. His novel 'A Family of Strangers' has been optioned for a major motion picture and he needs to fly east in January to meet with the talented director who has taken the option. Stuart Rosenberg, in the midst of directing "Murder Inc." an expose of the 1930's gang of killers for hire, has insisted Joe write the screenplay and he needs several days to guide Joe in the right direction. Reluctantly Joe agrees, a decision which he will quickly rue when he finds himself up to his belly button with drug dealers, loan sharks, Mafia hit men, wannabe Broadway stars and an up and coming New York actor named Peter Falk who may be on the verge of stardom. Someone has beaten drug dealer Gino Finucci to death and left his body in the basement of The Mudhole, an off-off-Broadway theater which is home to Amythyst Breen, a one time darling of Broadway struggling to find her way back to the top and also Jonathan Harker, slimy and ambitious, an actor caught in the grip of drug addiction even as he struggles to get that one lucky break that will propel him to stardom. Even as Joe fights to remain above the fray, he can feel himself being inexorably drawn into the intrigue of underworld vendettas culminating in a face to face confrontation with Carlo Gambino, the boss of bosses, and the most powerful Mafia chieftain in New York City.

## Book Fifteen—1961
## APPLE ANNIE AND THE DUDE

Joe Bernardi is a sucker for a sad story and especially when it comes from an old pal like Lila James who, after years of trying, has landed a plum assignment as a movie publicist. Frank Capra has okayed her for his newest film, A Pocketful of Miracles, now shooting on the Paramount lot. Get this right and her little company has a big future which is when God intervenes by inflicting her with a broken leg which will put her out of commission for at least a couple of weeks. Enter Joe as Sir Galahad to save the day and fill in. A simple favor, you say? Not so fast. First he'll have to deal with Heather Leeds, Lila's assistant, an ambitious tart in the mold of Eve Harrington, a devious cupcake who makes enemies the way Betty Crocker makes biscuits. Making his job even more difficult are the on-set feuds between Bette Davis and Glenn Ford with Capra getting migraines trying to referee. And then the fun really starts as a mysterious woman named Claire Philby from Northwestern University shows up to give Heather an award and maybe something else she never bargained for. Who killed Heather Leeds? Was it Philby or maybe Heather's husband Buddy Lovejoy, a struggling television writer, or perhaps even his writing partner, Seth Donnelley. And what about Heather's ex-husband Travis Wright who was just released from prison and claims Heather owes him $9,000,000 which he left in her care? Of more concern to Joe is the shadow of suspicion that has fallen on Dexter Craven, an old friend from the Warner Bros. days. Good old Lila, she's lying peacefully in a hospital bed while Joe deals with a nest of vipers, one of which is a cold blooded killer, and a movie in the making which is being tattered by conflicting egos. It's enough to make a man long for happier days when he was slogging through muddy France at the tail-end of World War II.

## Book Sixteen—1962
## 'TILL DEATH US DO PART

Who would want to kill a sweet old guy like Mike O'Malley, the prop master on Universal's "To Kill a Mockingbird"? Nobody, but dead he is, the victim of a hit and run that looks more like deliberate murder than accidental death. More likely the killer was after Mike's grandson Rory who had earned the enmity of Hank Greb, a burly mean-spirited teamster as well as Wayne Daniels, a wannabe actor, who claims erroneously that Rory's carelessness caused his face to be disfigured. Is this any of Joe Bernardi's business? Not really but when he showed up on the Mockingbird set as a favor to his hospitalized partner, Bertha Bowles, to woo newcomer William Windom to join the Bowles & Bernardi management firm, Joe was sucked into the situation right up to his tonsils, something he had little time for since his first priority was handling publicity for 'Lilies of the Field', a Sidney Poitier film, shooting in Tucson. Meanwhile Joe, who longs to write a second novel, has become increasingly bored with working at movie promotion and publicity. A twist of fate finds him befriended by Truman Capote and by Harper Lee who, like Joe, is trying to find that elusive second novel. Both are huge admirers of Joe's highly praised first novel and vow to help Joe get it made as a motion picture, even as Joe tries to expose the truth about Mike O'Malleys' death.

## Book Seventeen—1963
## CUE THE CROWS

How do you make a movie when the star of your dreams, eager to sign, is suddenly faced with a murder charge and could spend the rest of his life cooped up in San Quentin? Joe Bernardi, author, screenwriter and possibly a co-producer, has traveled north along the California coastline to Bodega Bay to hobnob with Rod Taylor who is filming Alfred Hitchcock's thriller, 'The Birds'. Rod is on the verge of signing the contract when a funny thing happens. The body of a young attractive redhead named Amanda Broome is found dead in the trunk of his Corvette. Taylor screams frame-up, even though Amanda has been stalking him for weeks and they had a violent and very public argument only hours before her body was discovered. Further filming of 'The Birds' is in jeopardy and so is the filming of Joe's movie based on his best-selling book. Looming large in the midst of this is Henrietta Boyle, a county attorney with gubernatorial ambitions and what better way to grease the path to the State House than to convict a famous movie star of homicide. But who else might have an interest in seeing Amanda dead? Perhaps her aunt, executrix of a trust fund which would have made Amanda a millionairess in a few short weeks. A definite possibility . Determined to prove Taylor innocent, Joe follows a trail that leads from a teen hangout in Palo Alto to the halls of academia to a posh country club where a triple A credit rating is the first requirement for membership. When a mysterious car tries to run Joe off the road into a deep and deadly crevasse in the hills above the Bay, he knows he's getting close to the truth but will the truth be revealed before Joe becomes buzzard bait?

## Book Eighteen—1964
## MURDER ABOARD THE HIGHLAND ROSE

The night was dark. Clouds obscured the moon. The elaborate yacht owned by Joseph Kennedy lay at anchor in Monterey Bay. Shortly past midnight a shot rang out. A man aboard the yacht had been murdered. The police ferried out to the boat and found nothing amiss and the next morning Kennedy's 'Highland Rose' continued its journey north to San Francisco. Rumors abounded and for thirty-five years the events of that night in 1929 have been hidden in mystery. And now it is 1964 and it has fallen to Joe Bernardi to solve the mystery and write the book that tells the truth about that terrible night. The rumored victim, an obscure talent agent named Archie Farrell. The rumored murderer, Joseph P. Kennedy himself. Witnesses to the rumored killing, film stars Gloria Swanson and Gladys George, writer Frances Marion, and producer Edward Albee, among others. And why, after thirty-five years, has the solution to this killing become so important? Because 1964 is an election year and John F. Kennedy will be running again for the Presidency. Will he succeed? There are those who hope he will not and they are working on a hatchet job, an expose of Joe Kennedy as a philanderer and a killer showing the President to be the seed of evil. Deadly forces array themselves against Joe in his quest for truth. It appears that the secret of the Highland Rose must be kept hidden at all costs while the fate of the country hangs in the balance.

Made in the USA
Monee, IL
15 October 2022

15925672R00125